SIOBHAN ROWDEN was born in Scotland and brought up in England. She has a degree in English and has worked as a holiday rep in Corfu, at Disney World in Florida and in a production company in London. The CURSE of the Bogle's Beard is her first novel. She lives in Brighton with her husband and children. She doesn't like beetroot or pickles.

THE CURSE OF THE Bogle's Beard

SIOBHAN ROWDEN

Illustrated by Mark Beech

SCHOLASTIC

First published in 2012 by Scholastic Children's Books
An imprint of Scholastic Ltd
Euston House, 24 Eversholt Street, London, NW1 1DB, UK
Registered office: Westfield Road, Southam, Warwickshire, CV47 0RA
SCHOLASTIC and associated logos are trademarks and/or
registered trademarks of Scholastic Inc.

Text © Siobhan Rowden, 2012
Illustrations © Mark Beech, 2012

ISBN 978 1407 12489 6

A CIP catalogue record for this book
is available from the British Library.

Printed by CPI Group (UK) Ltd, Croydon, CR0 4YY
Papers used by Scholastic Children's Books are made
from wood grown in sustainable forests.

1 3 5 7 9 10 8 6 4 2

This is a work of fiction. Names, characters, places, incidents
and dialogues are products of the author's imagination or are
used fictitiously. Any resemblance to actual people, living or dead,
events or locales is entirely coincidental.

www.scholastic.co.uk/zone

For Charlie, Harry and Katie

Prologue

Barnaby Figg couldn't tear his eyes away from the sight of the old woman in the enormous glass jar. Clumps of grey hair swam around her face before setting like jellied eels. Her dress twisted like a hungry snake around her legs and large belly.

Barnaby was transfixed, unaware of his own injuries. Her already wrinkled face was creased beyond all recognition, and two hooded eyes, full of anger and resentment, glared accusingly at him. He stared back at what now resembled a large and demented pickled walnut. It isn't nice to be hated by a walnut, especially a large and demented one.

He tried to look away, but realized with a jolt that he couldn't. Granny had been right – pickling was in his blood, and he had just been involved in the darkest pickling of all.

CHAPTER 1
The Purple Mansion

Four Days Earlier. . .

Barnaby opened his eyes and stared up at the revolting violet ceiling. He closed them again tightly, trying to shut out the hideous lilacs and mauves that surrounded him. He was staying in one of his Granny Hogsflesh's many bedrooms in her enormous mansion, in the middle of town. Everything was a shade of purple. It made her feel sophisticated, but it made Barnaby feel sick. He tried to imagine he was back in his little bed at home. His old bedroom was about the same size as the bed he was lying in now; in fact, the whole of his house could fit into just one of Granny's bedrooms. He loved his home. It was just outside of town by the Forest of Fen, and he was happy there. But then his dad left them.

Barnaby had watched him go from his bedroom window. His dad had pushed his collar up against the driving rain, pulled his pea green hat down firmly on his head, slipped through the garden gate and disappeared into the forest, checking over his shoulder as he went. Barnaby had no idea that would be the last time he would see him. But the hours turned into days, and the days to weeks. Eventually with no word from him and little money left, Barnaby's mum packed up a few of their possessions and moved in with her mother, Granny Hogsflesh. Granny pronounced her name *Ho-flay*, but everyone knew she was really a "Hogs-flesh".

"BARNABY?"

His eyes flew open as a rattling screech from the hall outside sent a wave of dread through his body.

"BARNABEEEE!"

It was her – Granny Hogsflesh.

"Barnaby, where are you, boy?"

"In my room, Granny Hogsflesh," he said, sitting up as the brass doorknob rattled. It was the shape and colour of a large pickled onion. All the doorknobs were. The onion turned and his grandmother stomped in.

"*Ho-flay*, boy, it is pronounced *Ho-flay*," she croaked. "What are you up to? You're going to be late for breakfast."

"I'm just . . . enjoying the view from my window."

Barnaby pointed towards a big red neon sign on a colossal factory opposite, smoke billowing out of its three massive chimneys.

Hogsflesh
Pickle Company

"Ah, yes," she whispered, and waddled over to look out. Her wrinkled old face was bathed in the red light and she looked like a fiendish prune. She was not much taller than Barnaby, but she was ten times wider. Bristly chins rippled down her heavy neck and joined the waves of flesh billowing out under her purple velvet dress, gathering at a huge belly.

"*Ho-flay* Pickles," she sighed.

She was dribbling slightly and a trickle had run down one of her chins, making her thick lips look like a pair of friendly slugs. She beckoned him over with a fleshy finger and he forced himself to take a step closer.

"One day, if you work hard and impress me, you could be the boss of all this," she said, waving a wobbly arm at the enormous factory. Barnaby glanced out of the window, and then over at his grandmother. She was bossy, loud and smelled of pickled cabbage. He didn't want to be any of those things.

"I'm not sure if I want to be a pickling boss, Granny," he said, quietly.

"Of course you do, you stupid boy. Pickling is in your blood."

She leaned closer and her vinegary breath enveloped him, making it hard to breathe.

"Your grandfather and I, God pickle his soul, built this empire up from nothing."

She was right next to him now and he staggered back, but she grabbed his arm.

"I'm not getting any younger, and the time has come to prepare my successor."

Barnaby tried to pull away, but his legs felt weak.

"I d-don't understand," he said.

"I need an heir, and your mother isn't interested. Your father turned her against the ancient art of pickling."

She snorted angrily, and a fine mist of spittle settled over Barnaby's face. "It's because of him she won't work in my factory. All she's interested in now is fresh produce. Ridiculous! Fresh food is just a fad. It will never last."

Barnaby wiped his face on his sleeve as Granny looked him up and down. "It would have been nice to have someone with a bit of spirit," she sniffed, "but unfortunately, you're all I have."

She was staring at him intently, still holding on to his arm. Then she pulled him close, stuck her long, cold nose in his ear and whispered, "You were born to pickle, Barnaby."

He felt sick. Having someone's nose in your ear is bad enough, but it's even worse when it belongs to your granny.

"Dad thinks I could be big in peas," he said, shakily.

Barnaby's dad was a pea picker, which meant plenty of peas, but not much money.

"Big in peas?" spat Granny, pushing him away from her. "Look where 'big in peas' gets you – my daughter and my grandson, abandoned in a shack with no money. Your father was a fool."

"It wasn't a shack," Barnaby said, struggling to hold back the tears. "And my dad wasn't a fool – I mean, he isn't a fool."

"Oh, you think he's coming back, do you? WELL, HE'S NOT," she yelled. "He's abandoned you and he's abandoned your mother. And that's why you have to live with me. So forget about him, forget about peas and start thinking pickles."

She walked towards the door.

"And don't be late for breakfast."

Then she left the room, the onion handle shaking as the door slammed.

CHAPTER 2
Footsteps

Barnaby slumped down on a chair by the window. His mouth was dry and he felt ill. His grandmother always had that effect on him. Before his dad left, he only had to visit her once a month for Sunday tea; now he would have to see her every day. He stared out at the red neon sign. Hogsflesh Pickles dominated the town and employed nearly everybody in it. Granny Hogsflesh was a very powerful and respected figure, although most people were terrified of her. Tears of frustration pricked Barnaby's eyes. He didn't want to be her heir; he didn't want her stupid pickle factory. He just wanted his dad back. Something must have happened; Dad would never abandon them like Granny said.

He opened a drawer and pulled out a tatty little book. He had seen it fall from his dad's pocket the night he watched him leave. By the time he had run into the garden to pick it up, his dad was long gone. It was an old diary belonging to some beetroot farmer. Barnaby had no idea why his dad had it, but he was keeping it safe, ready to return it to him.

Barnaby turned the little diary over in his hands. It had been two weeks since his dad had disappeared, and he was beginning to wonder whether he would ever come home. He opened the front cover and had another look.

The writing inside was neat but childish and very faded. There was a name and a date in the top corner of the first page. The year was so faint he couldn't read it, but he could just make out the name – Mary . . . something.

January 1st 19⬤
No holiday for me, even though it is New Year's Day. Father asked me to make a delivery to Mrs Cave-Brown-Cave. My arms are aching. Ten jars she wanted. Who in their right mind eats ten jars of beetroot? Thank goodness she does, though. No one else seems to like the stuff and that isn't good news for beetroot farmers. Still, it's my birthday soon. Maybe Mother will give me some time off. My hands are purple and I can't get rid of the smell.

Barnaby sighed. The diary was boring, and clearly wasn't going to tell him where his dad went, no matter how many times he read it. He threw the book across the room and it skidded out of sight. He pulled his knees up to his chin, wishing he had stood up to Granny more. His dad was always standing up to her. He wasn't willing to be controlled by her like everyone else. That's why he refused to work at Hogsflesh Pickles, much to Granny's annoyance. But Barnaby wasn't brave like his dad. He was just a short, quiet boy, who never said boo to a goose, and with his dad gone, he knew he would never have the courage.

Barnaby stood up as the sound of footsteps clomped along the corridor and stopped outside his room.

"Oh no, not again," he groaned, making his way over and opening the door. But the hall was empty.

"Granny?" he shouted. "Mum. . . Anyone?"

No reply. He closed the door. Very strange. . .

"This place is making me go mad," he muttered, climbing on the huge purple bed. He pulled the covers over his head, trying to ignore the picture of a pickled onion and egg embossed on the pillowcases. How long would they have to stay here?

A gentle voice drifted under the duvet.

"Barnaby?"

It was his mum.

"Come in," he called.

Barnaby suddenly felt much better as he watched her coming through the door. Hatty Figg was small with dark, curly hair and would have been very pretty if it weren't for a single thick brown hair that protruded from her chin. Barnaby had seen her pulling it out every morning, but it always grew back again.

"Were you here just a minute ago?" he asked.

"No," she said.

"I thought I heard footsteps."

"Must be the bogles," she whispered, with a smile.

She always said that. Whenever they couldn't find something, whenever there was an odd noise, that sort of thing, she blamed "the bogles". Barnaby was annoyed she wasn't taking him seriously.

"Why do you always say that?" he asked, grumpily. "We both know there are no such things as bogles."

"I'm sorry," she sighed. "It's just a silly thing that Granny used to say when she couldn't explain something. It used to make you laugh when you were little."

"Well, I'm not little any more. I'm ten, so stop saying it."

Mum sighed again and sat down on the bed. She put her arm around him.

"It's been a tough couple of weeks," she said, "but this is only temporary, Barnaby. I'm sure your dad just needed some time alone and will be back soon."

"Why did he leave?" he asked. "Was it because he lost his job at the pea farm?"

He looked up into his mum's worried face.

"I've been to see Dad's boss, Mr Pottage, the owner of the pea farm," she said. "He said your dad had been behaving very strangely. They had an argument, but he is willing to give him his job back. He also said that Dad was visited at the farm the day before by a weird little woman."

"What did he mean, 'weird'?"

"Well, he was very unkind and said she looked like a hairy beetroot with legs."

Barnaby giggled.

"It's not funny," said Mum. "It was just after that, all the trouble started."

Barnaby thought back to the days before his dad left. He had come home from work one night looking extremely odd, with dark shadows under his eyes and several gruesome hairs hanging from his unshaven chin. His normally floppy red hair was standing on end and he had burped his way through dinner, picked his nose, wiped it on the table and disappeared into the bedroom without a word.

"It was so unlike him," frowned Mum. "He hates burping."

"Is that why you do it quietly?" asked Barnaby.

Mum turned pink.

"I do not burp," she said. "It's hiccups."

Barnaby said nothing, but she was always making strange windy noises when she thought no one was listening.

"It's a medical condition," she continued. "There's nothing I can do about it."

"I like burping," said Barnaby. "I can do it louder than anyone in my whole school."

"Well, don't," she said. "Your father wouldn't like it. Although he certainly wouldn't have cared the last time we saw him. . ."

She broke off and stared down at the floor.

"He's all right, isn't he, Mum?" asked Barnaby.

She looked up at him and stroked a strand of hair away from his face.

"Don't you worry about Dad," she said. "Sometimes, grown-ups just need a little time on their own. He'll come home soon and we'll be back in our own house before you know where you are."

Barnaby started to relax.

"And remember what your dad said before all this started?"

It seemed so long ago that he couldn't think what his dad had said.

"He said you could have a dog," she said. "In fact, we can ask Granny if we can get one while we're here."

Barnaby's grin was almost as wide as the bed. He desperately wanted a dog.

"But now it's time for you to get dressed. You don't want to be late for breakfast."

She smiled and left the room.

Barnaby hurriedly pulled his clothes on and walked down to the breakfast room feeling much happier. Everything was going to be OK. His dad was coming back, they would leave Granny's house, go home and get a dog – brilliant.

But Barnaby was wrong. That was not what was going to happen at all.

CHAPTER 3
Pickled Breakfast

Granny Hogsflesh and Mum were already sitting at a long table, having a heated conversation while eating their pickled gherkins on toast. Barnaby slipped in quietly. Breakfast was laid out across the table. Pickled eggs, pickled onions, pickled Brussels sprouts, gherkins and toast. He groaned and helped himself to some toast.

"Get a dog? Not on my nelly," slurped Granny, drinking her tea. "Nasty, vile creatures, with stinking breath," she spluttered, "slobbering all over my furniture."

Barnaby glanced at his grandmother as he sat down at the table. *She would have a lot in common with a dog*, he thought. She caught his eye and held it, slowly wiping her wet mouth with a napkin. He looked away, certain she had read his thoughts.

"But, Mother, it would just be until Fergus comes back and then we can all go home," pleaded his mum. "Poor Barnaby's been through so much recently, it would cheer him up no end."

Granny continued looking at Barnaby, and then down at his plate of toast.

"Where are your pickles?" she demanded.

"Erm. . . I'm not very hungry, Granny."

"You can't start the day without any pickles," she said. "Get some. Honestly, Hatty, no pickles? No wonder the boy is so feeble."

Barnaby reluctantly helped himself to a slippery gherkin and a slimy pickled egg.

"It's about time you two realized, that man is never coming back," continued Granny. "Now he's out of the way, you need to get yourselves down to the factory with me and start learning the family business. It's because of him that my daughter and my grandson aren't interested in pickles – it's humiliating."

"It is not because of him," said Mum. "You know I have never been interested in pickling, Mother. And as for Barnaby, he can work with you if he wants. But it's totally up to him."

Barnaby hid behind his gherkin and pulled a face.

"Anyway," continued his mum, "I already

have a job – in fresh produce."

Granny made a horrible grunting noise and started stabbing her pickled egg with a fork.

"Got a job? Who'd have you?" she snapped.

"Mr Pottage, the owner of the pea farm, has kindly overlooked the incidents with Fergus and allowed me to take over his job until his return."

"Then you'll be there for ever, you stupid girl," fumed Granny, "because he's not coming back."

"Yes, he is," said Mum, standing up. "And Barnaby and I are only staying here until I get enough money together for us to return home. But we can always leave earlier."

Barnaby's heart leapt. They were going sooner than he thought. But Granny looked alarmed.

"You are so stubborn, Hatty *Ho-flay*," she said. "I don't know where you get it from."

"It's Hatty Figg, Mother, and has been since

the day I married my husband," said Mum, glaring at Granny. "And I know exactly where I get my stubbornness from."

Granny started shovelling the demolished egg into her mouth.

"Sit down and tell me what happened at that pea farm," she said, spraying yolk across the table. "Why did that husband of yours lose his job?"

Barnaby was sure he saw a slight smile as she asked the question.

"It wasn't really his fault," said Mum, slightly flustered. "He hadn't been himself since the day he came home late from work. Something must have happened that day."

"What do you mean, 'he wasn't quite himself'?" Granny asked, her big lips still twitching.

"He was very agitated and snappy," continued Mum. "He seemed unable to control his behaviour – belching, burping and generally being extremely rude. He wouldn't wash or shave and grew the most horrible beard in just two days. Didn't he, Barnaby?"

Barnaby nodded slowly, and shuddered at the thought of the thick black hairs that curled down his dad's chin like a nest of dead spiders.

"Everything came to a head when Mr Pottage accused him of flicking peas at his colleagues and ignoring health and safety regulations with his . . . er . . . windiness in the pea preparation area," said Mum. "They had an argument and Fergus was sent home." She looked down at her uneaten Brussels sprouts. "If he doesn't contact us soon, I'm going to have to go to the police."

There was a great choking sound as Granny Hogsflesh coughed up her breakfast.

"There's no need for that," she spluttered. "Unfortunately, there's no law against abandoning your family."

"My husband would never—"

"Anyway," interrupted Granny. "What about the boy? Who's going to look after him all through the summer holidays?"

"He can come with me," said Mum. "There's plenty for him to do at the farm and he can earn some pocket money."

"I don't think so," said Granny, staring at him. "I will give him a holiday job at the factory. That will be much better."

Barnaby didn't want a job at the pea farm or at the pickle factory.

"Can I be excused?" he asked, trying to hide the pickles under his half-eaten toast.

"No, you can't," said Granny, looking suspiciously at his plate. "What are you going to do all day?" She glared at him. "I'm working from home today – I've got some work to do in the cellar – and I don't want you getting under my feet."

"What's in the cellar?" he asked.

Granny Hogsflesh leaned across the table and fixed him with an unblinking stare.

"You are not to come anywhere near that cellar," she hissed.

It felt like a threat, and Barnaby glanced up at his mum, but she was busy helping herself to some more toast.

"W – why?" he breathed.

"There are things down there that would turn your blood to ice," she whispered. "Dangerous things, not for the eyes of children. Do you understand, boy?"

"Yes, Granny," he said, shifting in his chair. She was still watching him closely. He had to think of something quickly to keep her happy. He forced a wet gherkin in his mouth and tried to smile. He rolled it around with his tongue, felt his stomach protest, but braced himself and bit down hard. It exploded, filling his mouth with bitter slivers of soggy pickle. He coughed, sending a stream of vinegar out of his nose and down his chin.

"Enjoy that, did you?" asked Granny.

Barnaby closed his eyes and swallowed.

"Yuck," he croaked, as it oozed down his throat.

Granny's eyes glinted dangerously.

"What did you say?" she whispered.

Barnaby realized he had made a terrible mistake.

"I mean . . . yup," he said, hurriedly. "Yup, I really enjoyed the, um, pickled thing. . . Mmm, delicious!"

Granny relaxed back in her chair as Barnaby gulped down a large glass of water.

"Well then, I think you should learn more about 'pickled things', as you call them," she said. "You can do some research in my library. That will keep you busy all day."

Barnaby sighed. It was going to be a long day.

Granny got up and stood behind his chair. She bent over so her head was next to his. He could smell the pickled eggs she'd just eaten.

"Time for my grandson to learn the basics of the business he was born into."

Her spongy wet lips smacked together and for one awful moment he thought she was going to kiss him. But she turned her face towards him and in went that long cold nose again, right in his ear, sending shivers of disgust down to his toenails.

"I'll take you there myself," she whispered.

CHAPTER 4
The Library

The library was a five-minute walk away from the mauve breakfast room. Granny led Barnaby down a lurid purple staircase to the lower ground floor.

"I've always wondered, why is everything in your house is a shade of purple?" he asked.

"It is the colour of royalty, Barnaby," she said, "a sign of noble blood. The queen's own house is full of purple . . . stuff."

"How do you know?"

"I know," she sniffed, "that the queen and I have very similar taste."

"Hmm," muttered Barnaby.

They walked along a wide corridor and past a narrow stone staircase which circled down to the cellar. A cold blast of air tousled Barnaby's hair as they went by; he suspected it wasn't mauve down there. What on earth did Granny Hogsflesh do in a cellar all day long? She caught his eye and fixed him with that icy stare again. He was sure she could read minds.

Eventually they came to an enormous set of double doors. Barnaby peered round his granny's bulky frame as she heaved one open. The ceiling was about seven metres high and the circular room was lined from top to bottom with books. A massive arched window was at the far end, with a round table in front. But it was the huge ladder attached to a track on the floor and a rail on the ceiling that Barnaby was staring at.

Granny
followed his
gaze. "Watch this," she
announced, picking up a small
remote control from the table.
"It's my railroad ladder – I've only
recently had it installed. Apparently the
queen has one too."

She climbed a short way up the long ladder,
pressed a button, and the whole thing, with
Granny on board, started to travel slowly around
the circular room on the track. It began picking

up speed.
Barnaby heard a
small shriek and thought
he saw a look of excitement
on his grandmother's face as her
skirt and hair started flying out behind
her. He stood in the middle of the room
watching her zooming round and round,
faster and faster.

"The harder you press, the quicker it goes,"
she yelled, her big tummy quivering with the
force. Barnaby started to worry that she was

going to fly off and crash into him, but he was also secretly impressed. He saw a new side to her – "adrenaline granny".

Eventually she slowed down and came to a stop.

"Can I have a go, Granny?"

"A go?" she panted. "It's not a toy, Barnaby. It's a highly engineered piece of . . . engineering, only to be used for reaching books on high shelves."

"But you were riding it for fun," he said.

"I never do anything for fun. Anyway, the pickling books are on the lower shelves, so you won't need the ladder."

She led him to the round table and picked out a thick manual.

"*Understanding Onions*," she said. "One of my personal favourites, but there are many more books if you finish this one. Now, I have work to do, but I'll be testing you tonight at dinner to see how much you have learned."

Then she turned and wobbled out of the door, her big bottom bouncing gently under her purple dress.

Barnaby stared at the front cover of *Understanding Onions* – a picture of a red onion, a white onion, a spring onion and a shallot. Surly that was all there was to understand about onions. He turned to the first page.

Introduction

Not many people are aware, but this pungent edible bulb comes from the lily family.

Barnaby yawned and closed the book. He spotted the remote control on the table beside him and wandered over to the railroad ladder. He stood at the bottom and looked up at the distant ceiling. It made him feel dizzy. Cautiously he climbed up on to the first rung, pushed the button and went once round the room very slowly before feeling slightly ill. He pulled out a book at the place he stopped: *Regal Rooms and Royal Refurbishment*. He sighed and put the book back and tried once more to get some speed up on the railroad ladder, but felt so queasy he had to stop again. "Pathetic," he muttered, climbing down. "Even my own grandmother is braver than me."

Barnaby wandered around the room several times before deciding that he had better learn something if he was going to be tested at dinner tonight. He got out several books and sat back down at the table. *Relish Your Relish* looked well thumbed, as did *The Pleasures of Pickling* and *Pickling Problems*. **The Big Book of Beetroot** was obviously very well used. It looked extremely old and was falling apart. He decided it must be a good one to look at, and glanced inside at the contents. A name had been written at the top of the page: Mary Morley. It looked vaguely familiar. The chapters listed underneath were:

Barnaby turned to the first chapter and glanced down at the different types of beetroot. It was so boring he couldn't bring himself to read it. He pushed the book away and let his head drop slowly until it was resting on the table. How was he going to manage all day in here? He should have gone to the pea farm with Mum. Now he was stuck in the library, and Granny was in the cellar with her "dangerous things". He sat up. What did she mean, "not for the eyes of children"? It couldn't hurt if he had a little listen at the door... He thought about it for a moment, then decided he wasn't brave enough to find out, and turned again to **The Big Book of Beetroot**. As he read about the different varieties, his eyelids began to droop, closely followed by his head and shoulders, until his nose touched one of the pages. It smelled terrible and he quickly pulled away. He couldn't do this all day; he needed some excitement. He had to face his fear.

Barnaby put the books back on the shelves and left the library, creeping along the corridor to the stone staircase which led down to the cellar. He shivered slightly and stopped for a moment. He could just make out a dim light way below. He desperately wanted to sneak down, but couldn't seem to make his legs move in that direction. Granny's words echoed in his ears: "dangerous things", "not for the eyes of children". He couldn't do it. She was right; he was feeble. He turned to go but stopped again. She didn't have to be right. It was up to him. Slowly he put one foot on the first stone step. He froze as he heard a loud pummelling sound, but soon realized it was his own heart and carried on until he reached the bottom. He stood before a great oak door and was surprised to see that it had a large key in the lock. Why would you leave a key in a door if you wanted to keep people out? He pressed his ear against the door but could hear nothing. All he had to do was turn the lock, push the door and peep inside. He reached a trembling hand towards the key.

Footsteps clattered on the other side of the cellar door. Barnaby panicked. He jerked his hand back, turned and bounded up the stone steps two at a time. He tore along the corridor, up the two flights of stairs towards his room and stopped outside, panting heavily. As his breathing returned to normal, he began to feel very annoyed with himself. Why did he get into such a state? It was just footsteps. "But at least I did it," he said to himself, "I made it down those steps and listened at the door."

It was a start.

Barnaby felt much better as he walked into his bedroom, but the feeling vanished the minute he stepped in.

CHAPTER 5
Ransacked

Barnaby's room had been wrecked. Drawers were pulled out, bedclothes thrown on the floor and books flung off the shelves. Barnaby cautiously walked in, checking the room was empty. Who would do this? Granny had a cleaner and a cook, but he doubted it was them. The cleaner hated any mess and the cook never left the kitchen. Mum wouldn't do it either, so that just left Granny herself – but why? She was very strict about keeping things tidy. Slowly he began to straighten the room out. Maybe she had heard him bounding up the stairs and left in a hurry;

but if it was her, then whose footsteps had he heard in the cellar? He knelt down to pick up a drawer, filling it with his scattered belongings. Could whoever it was be looking for something? But he didn't have anything. Most of his stuff was back at his old house. He picked up a couple of bouncy balls, a paper plane, and reached under the wardrobe to get some coloured pens that had rolled beneath. His hand touched a book and he pulled out the old diary he had thrown across the room earlier. He stared at it for a moment. Why did his dad have this book? Maybe he should

read it, no matter how boring it was. Barnaby turned to the second page.

January 2nd
It's my birthday tomorrow. Every year I get a present made from beetroot. I'm not complaining. When I was little I had a dolly made from beetroot called Beatrix, which I loved. I know we have no money and it's the best they can do. But I will be eighteen. Surely they can't give me dollies, balls and board games made from beetroot any more? They only rot away after a few years, anyway.

January 3rd
Feeling very guilty about earlier comments. I am so excited. Have been given a book, my first ever book – The Big Book of Beetroot.

Barnaby stopped reading. He flicked back to the smudged name on the inside cover. He could just make it out – Mary Morley – the same name that was inside **The Big Book of Beetroot**, which now belonged to Granny Hogsflesh. Who was Mary Morley? Dad had her diary and Granny had her beetroot book. Maybe the diary and **The Big Book of Beetroot** weren't that boring after all.

Barnaby raced back to the library, the diary still in his hands, pulled out **The Big Book of Beetroot** and sat at the round table under the window. He opened the front cover. There was the name, in the same childish handwriting in the top corner – Mary Morley. Maybe there was a clue in here that could lead to his dad.

VARIETIES
Burpees Golden
Red Ace
Boltardy
Pablo
Albina Vereduna

Barnaby couldn't face reading about different types of beetroot again and he was sure it couldn't possibly help. He turned to the next chapter.

RECIPES
Beef and Beetroot Stew
Pink Mash
Borscht Soup
Beetroot and Onion Chutney
Chocolate Beetroot Cake

The list went on. Barnaby didn't know what he was looking for, but he was beginning to think that this was a waste of time. Next chapter.

FOLKLORE
Greek Mythology
The Oracle at Delphi pronounced that the beetroot was worth its weight in silver. Even Aphrodite, the Goddess of Love, ate beetroot to retain her beauty.

Roman Legend
The Romans believed that if a man and woman ate from the same beetroot, they would fall in love.

Norse Mythology
Beetroot was used to make Kvas – "the drink of knowledge".

Each legend went on in depth and there were certainly a lot of cultures who believed that beetroot was pretty potent stuff, but none of this was of any help. He glanced at the final chapter.

MEDICINAL
Beet juice put into the nostrils can relieve toothache and foul breath.

Granny Hogsflesh could do with a beetroot up her nose, Barnaby thought. He was still looking down the list when the double doors swung open and in thudded his grandmother.

"Just checking how you're getting on, Barnaby," she said.

As she sat down a big belch rumbled inside her, eventually escaping through her long teeth in a low hiss.

"Well, tell me what you've read this morning," she demanded.

"I've been learning all about beetroot, Granny," said Barnaby, feeling sick again.

He swung **The Big Book of Beetroot** round towards her. Her face dropped when she saw it.

"Where did you get this?" she asked, in a low voice. Barnaby was sure he saw her hand tremble as she flicked to the inside cover and read the faded name at the top.

"Here in the library," he said, watching her closely. "And I've found out that beetroot juice can cure bad breath," he added, hopefully.

"Stuff and nonsense," cried Granny, slamming the book shut. "If you took any notice of my business, you would know that I don't pickle beetroot in my factory."

"Oh . . . yes . . . of course," he said, uncertainly. He didn't want to make her any more upset than she already was, but he had to ask why.

"So . . . what's wrong with beetroot, then?"

"No one likes beetroot," she snapped. "It's a waste of time and effort – horrible, nasty stuff."

She got up to go, holding the book.

"I didn't realize this old thing was still around. After lunch, why don't you read *Pick a Piccalilli* instead of this nonsense?" She pulled out a book and handed it to him.

She glanced at **The Big Book of Beetroot**, then tucked it firmly under her arm and marched out of the library.

Barnaby put down *Pick a Piccalilli* and pulled the diary out of his pocket, staring at the cover. Granny was clearly not happy to see **The Big Book of Beetroot**. She had confiscated one book belonging to Mary Morley, would she take the diary away too if she knew he had it? He had to find out exactly who this Mary Morley was.

CHAPTER 6
The Stolen Baby

Barnaby slipped the diary in between the covers of *Pick a Piccalilli* in case Granny returned unexpectedly, then he began to read.

January 4th
Have learned lots of interesting things from my beetroot book. Am going to make beef and beetroot stew tonight (without the beef) as a thank-you to Mother and Father. Followed by chocolate and beetroot cake (without the chocolate). Folklore and myths also very interesting.

January 5th

Very odd thing happened to me today. I was in the pickling shed when I heard a strange high-pitched crying outside. There under the beetroot rows wrapped in a shawl was the strangest creature. It was purple and ugly and reminded me of my old beetroot dolly Beatrix. I picked it up and it stopped crying. It's a baby something, but not sure what. Gave it some of our milk. Am hiding it from Mother, I know she won't let me keep it.

January 6th

What a dreadful day. Mother discovered the baby thing and was horrified. I'll never forget the look on her face. I tried to explain that I was only trying to help as the poor thing had been abandoned in the beetroot. She kept saying that we had to return it. I asked her where to, but just then I found out. The strangest person appeared at the door. She was about four feet tall with a huge belly. I could tell she was female despite the hairy chin. She was shrieking at me to give back her baby. I tried to apologize but she wouldn't listen, her purple face screwed up in rage. Then she grabbed her child, pointed a long bony finger at me and screeched, "I curse you with . . . the bogle's beard."

Bogles! Barnaby looked back at the diary's description of the baby's mother — four feet tall, hairy chin and purple face; and the baby looked like a beetroot. The words "hairy beetroot on legs" came back to him. It was his dad's boss Mr Pottage's description of the strange little woman who had visited his dad at the pea farm. He had to find out exactly what a bogle was and he was in the right place – a huge library.

Barnaby spent the rest of the afternoon scouring the bookshelves for reference books on myths, legends or fairytales. But there was nothing. Most of the books were either about pickling or the royal family. He didn't quite reach the highest shelves; he couldn't face climbing to the top of the railroad ladder, let alone moving around on it. After hours of hunting he gave up. It was nearly dinner time and he would ask his mum. She was always on about bogles; maybe she would know.

That evening at dinner Barnaby sat between Mum and Granny and told them both about the state he had found his bedroom in. He didn't take his eyes away from his granny's face as he talked, watching her reaction closely. He could just make out small beads of sweat appearing on her top lip. She looked away from him and hesitated before turning to his mum.

"Really, Hatty," she muttered. "You need to teach that boy to look after his stuff and keep his room tidy in my house."

"Barnaby's normally very good," said Mum, uncertainly.

"Of course it was him," said Granny. "Who else would do it? Now, I don't want to hear another word about it. I want to hear all about Barnaby's pickling research today."

He knew she was trying to change the subject, but it didn't matter. It was clearly no surprise to her that somebody had been in his room. So it was either her, or she knew who had done it.

"Well, Barnaby," said Granny. "Tell us all about piccalilli."

Barnaby had been so engrossed in the diary and searching the library for any information on bogles that he had forgotten to look at the piccalilli book. He didn't even know what it was. He suddenly felt nervous as Granny's full attention turned on him.

"Well . . . it's pickled," he began.

"Of course it's pickled, you great nincompoop. What else?"

"It has lilies in it?" he asked, feeling panicky.

"It has what in it?" Granny's voice got louder and she looked at him suspiciously. He couldn't let her know he hadn't been reading up on pickles all afternoon; she would want to know what he had been up to.

"Well . . . it has onions in . . . and not many people are aware, but this pungent edible bulb comes from the lily family . . . and so in a way, it has lilies in it."

She was still looking at him. He tried to stop his clammy hands from fidgeting. But then a thick smile slowly pushed its way through Granny's wrinkles.

"I never thought of it like that," she said. "I like it Barnaby, I like it. You're not as brainless as you look."

She got up and walked round the table to him. Oh no, he thought, not the nose in the ear again. She was bearing down on him. He had to stop her. He opened his mouth to speak, but he didn't know what to say. The smell of her pickled breath was closing in. Her long nose was edging towards his small ear. He had to act fast.

"Mary Morley!" he blurted.

It had the right effect. Granny stopped abruptly, her face turning pale.

"Who?" asked his mum.

"Mary Mor—"

"Never heard of her," interrupted Granny, returning to her chair.

"I was just wondering who she was," said Barnaby, innocently. "Her name was on the inside cover of **The Big Book of Beetroot**."

"The big book of what?" asked his mum.

"Never heard of her," Granny repeated. "I got that book in a charity shop; it must have been the previous owner."

"But, Mother, you never go into charity shops."

"Right, I've got a busy day ahead of me tomorrow," she said, completely ignoring her daughter and getting up to go. "I shall see you both in the morning."

Barnaby watched her trundling towards the door. She knew exactly who Mary Morley was, he was sure of it. And his dad had known too. There was a connection between them all, and he intended to find out exactly what it was.

CHAPTER 7
Going Mad

As the door banged shut behind Granny Hogsflesh, Barnaby turned to his mum.

"She's lying," he said. "She knows who Mary Morley is."

"A name you found in a big book of. . .?"

"Beetroot," said Barnaby. "And she knows who messed up my room."

Mum got up and walked around the long table to sit down next to him.

"Are you sure you didn't leave your room in a mess, Barnaby?" she asked, taking hold of his hand. "You haven't been yourself lately and I don't blame you for that."

"Mum, it wasn't me," he cried. "It's her! I think she might have something to do with Dad going missing."

"Oh Barnaby, don't be so ridiculous," said Mum. "I know you miss your dad – we both do – but you can't blame Granny."

"Well, she's definitely up to something. She told me there were dangerous things in the cellar. What is she hiding down there?"

"She's not hiding anything. It's where she does some sort of experimental pickling," said Mum. "The 'dangerous things' are just the chemicals and pickling agents she uses. The cellar's linked to the pickle factory by an underground tunnel."

"Experimental pickling?" repeated Barnaby. "What does that mean?"

"I'm not sure. No one is allowed in there."

"No one?" he said. "Not one single person?"

Mum shook her head.

"So she's got something down there. . ." said Barnaby, thinking aloud, "something that she doesn't want anyone to know about."

A horrible thought crawled into his head and he gasped out loud.

"What's wrong?" asked Mum.

"What if she's got Dad down there?"

"Listen to me, Barnaby," sighed Mum. "Granny has nothing to do with Dad's disappearance. I know she's bossy and burpy, but she does love us . . . she just has a strange way of showing it."

"You can say that again," said Barnaby. "And she certainly doesn't love Dad; she hates him."

"She doesn't *hate* him . . . much. And she certainly wouldn't or couldn't lock him up in the cellar. Your dad is about twice as tall as she is, for starters."

Barnaby relaxed. He was overreacting.

"Granny just wants him to work for her like everyone else," continued Mum. "And you know what your dad is like – fiercely independent. He doesn't want to be controlled by her like the rest of the town. And neither do I, but that doesn't mean I don't want to spend some time with her. She is my mother, even if she is extremely annoying."

"I suppose mothers can be very annoying sometimes," smiled Barnaby.

Mum gasped in fake disapproval, and then smiled back.

"Anyway," she said, "who is this Mary Morley, and what has she got to do with anything?"

Barnaby was tempted to tell her about the diary, but she might show it to Granny. And if she took it away, like *The Big Book of Beetroot*, he would never find out who Mary Morley was or what happened to her.

"It's just a name I found in an old book in Granny's library," he said. "But I think Dad might know who she is. And judging by Granny's reaction just now, I think she does too. There's a connection, but I don't know what it is yet."

"That doesn't mean Granny has anything to do with your dad going missing," said Mum. "You know she wouldn't do anything bad."

"I don't," said Barnaby. "I don't know much about her at all."

Mum sighed.

"Maybe that's my fault," she said. "Maybe we should have visited more than just once a month."

"No!" cried Barnaby. "Once a month is more than enough. All she ever does is call me stupid and feeble. But I would like to know more about her."

"Well, I suppose now is the perfect time," said

Mum, "while we're staying here. What would you like to know?"

Barnaby thought for a moment. "What was Grandpa Hogsflesh like?"

Mum sat back in her chair. "He was a lovely man, died before you were born, but you knew that. He absolutely adored me . . . and your granny."

She smiled as Barnaby pulled a face.

"They grew up together on neighbouring farms," she continued.

Barnaby jumped up.

"Mary Morley also grew up on a farm – a beetroot farm," he said, excitedly.

"They weren't beetroot farmers," said Mum. "Grandpa was an onion farmer and Granny was a chicken farmer, before they started pickling his onions and her eggs."

"Oh," said Barnaby, feeling disappointed.

"But Granny hates beetroot and Mary was a beetroot farmer – that's a link."

"Why do you need to find a link between Granny and Mary Morley?" asked Mum.

"I just want to know more about Granny. What's wrong with that?"

"Why don't you ask her yourself? You can get to know her properly while we're staying here. I think she's desperate to show you round the factory."

Barnaby screwed up his face. He didn't want to spend any more time with Granny than was absolutely necessary.

"I'm not interested in the factory," he said. "I want to be a pea picker, just like Dad."

Mum ruffled his hair.

"You'll make a great pea picker," she said. "Although I'm not sure your granny will approve."

"Tell me more about her," he said.

"Well, let me see . . . her first name is Beatrix."

Barnaby had never thought of his granny having a name before. She was just Granny Hogsflesh.

"What else?"

"Well . . . I didn't really see much of her when I was a child. She was so busy building her pickle industry that I was mainly brought up by my dad. She wasn't very maternal – you're not the only one to be called stupid all the time. I don't think she means to be mean; it's just the way she is."

"But you're not like that," said Barnaby.

"No," said Mum, giving him a squeeze. "I'm making up for all the cuddles I never got."

"What was her mum like?" he asked.

"Hmm, I'm not sure; Granny never talks about her parents. They died long before I was born."

"What were they called?"

"I don't know, I would have to find that out," she said. "Her grandparents brought her up."

"Don't you want to know what your grandparents were called?" urged Barnaby.

"Maybe, but it's getting late now, so no more questions. Come on, up to bed."

They made their way slowly up to his room. Barnaby's head was buzzing with questions, but he kept them to himself. He still had a hunch that Granny might have something to do with Dad going missing. He had to find out more about her.

Mum wasn't much help. She hardly knew anything at all about her own mother. Maybe he should get to know Granny himself. If he pretended to be interested in her horrible pickles, he might get a few answers; he might even get to find out what was in the cellar.

"One more thing," Barnaby said, as they reached his door. "I need to find out exactly what a bogle is."

"Bogles? Why do you want to know about bogles?"

"Trust me, Mum. They might not be as imaginary as we think. Mr Pottage said someone strange visited the pea farm just before Dad went missing."

"Of course they are imaginary. They are small, hairy, made up. . ." She stopped and examined Barnaby's face. "Please don't tell me you think a bogle visited your dad."

He shrugged.

"Barnaby, look at me," she said, cupping his face in her hands. "Bogles are not real, and Granny has not locked your dad up in the cellar. You have been through a rough few weeks and you need some rest. Go to bed, have a good night's sleep and we'll talk in the morning. OK, my love?"

It was no use saying any more. His mum obviously thought he was going mad and maybe she was right.

CHAPTER 8
Getting Into Pickles

The next day at breakfast Granny Hogsflesh announced it was time for Barnaby to learn more about the family business first-hand. He felt nervous but excited. This was the perfect opportunity to find out all about her.

"You may not be interested in pickling, Hatty, but Barnaby will be," she said, glaring at her daughter. "He did some excellent work in the library yesterday."

"I think Barnaby would prefer to be a pea picker," said Mum, "just like his dad."

"If his dad had listened to me and joined my

pickling empire, he might be here now," said Granny.

There was a tense silence as Mum thought about what Granny had just said. She glanced at Barnaby and he tried to give her an "I told you so" look.

"What exactly do you mean by that, Mother?" asked Mum.

There was another uncomfortable pause before Granny said, "I simply mean that you would have plenty of money, plenty of food and live in a big house like mine, rather than that shed you called a home."

"Why do you say these things?" cried Mum, getting to her feet. "It isn't a shed, it is our home and we were happy there."

"So happy that he left you," snapped Granny.

Mum sank back down on her chair, a bewildered look on her face.

"I don't understand," she said quietly. "He changed, almost overnight. One day he was his usual happy self, the next he was surly and rude and refusing to wash and shave, and the next he was gone."

Barnaby got up and put his arm around her.

He looked up at the sound of Granny shifting uncomfortably in her chair. She was staring at Mum with a strange look on her face. She caught him looking at her and turned away.

"You're much better off without him," she murmured. "Here with me."

"No, we are not," said Mum. "Why must you always say these horrible things? Barnaby, get your coat, you're coming with me to the pea farm today. It won't be long before I have enough money together for us to return to 'that shed'."

"Actually, Mum," said Barnaby, quietly, "if it's OK, I *would* like to find out more about pickling."

Mum's eyebrows shot up and Granny Hogsflesh looked triumphant. Barnaby gave his mum a hug and said loudly, "You get off to work and I'll see you tonight."

Then he whispered, "It's OK, I know what I'm doing." He gave her a reassuring smile as she left the room, and then turned to face his grandmother.

Granny looked at Barnaby from across the table as she gulped down her tea. Another big burp rolled around her vast belly, making her chins ripple before bursting out with a loud phlegmy

BRRRRUUUURRRRPHPHPH!

"Maybe you're not a feeble-minded little twerp after all," she said, clearing her throat. "Well, where shall we start, young man?"

"The cellar?" asked Barnaby, tentatively.

She frowned. "Is that the reason for your sudden interest in pickles? So you can go prying in my cellar?"

"No, Granny . . . I was just . . . it was just . . . after reading *Pick a Piccalilli* . . . great read."

Granny seemed to relax again. "Yes, truly inspiring, isn't it?"

"Um . . . yeah . . . amazing," said Barnaby, his cheeks turning pink.

"So no more talk of the cellar," she said. "You're not ready for that yet, but I'll be watching you closely from now on. We will know when the time is right."

Barnaby didn't know exactly what that meant, but decided it was best not to ask too many questions.

"We will start off in the factory," she said, standing up. "Come on, we don't want to miss the company anthem, and I have a speech to deliver to my workers this morning."

They made their way along the hall to the two huge front doors. Granny stopped to put on her hat and gloves. It wasn't cold, but she always insisted on putting them on to walk the two minutes from her house to the factory.

"A lady should never leave the house without proper attire," she said, burping loudly.

It was the silliest little hat that balanced on top of her head like a paper cup, with a long purple feather poking out of it.

Barnaby tried not to giggle as she checked her reflection in the mirror and pulled on her purple satin gloves.

"One never knows who one could meet when one goes out," she said.

Barnaby noticed that she tended to talk like that the minute she put her little hat on.

When she was ready, he turned towards the big double doors. Instead of onion handles, these had long silver gherkins on each side. Just as Barnaby was reaching for one, he thought he heard someone softly calling his name.

"*Barnaby. . .*"

He spun around but the hall was empty.

"What was that?" he asked.

"I didn't hear anything," said Granny, squeezing through the door.

"I heard a voice," he said.

"It must have been the cleaner. Now come

along or we shall be late."

"But it didn't sound human; it was strange."

She was trying to look calm, but Barnaby could tell she was agitated.

"Then it must have been the wind. It escapes up from the cellar and rattles around the corridors."

Barnaby looked at her doubtfully, but said no more. He needed to keep her happy if he was to find out anything.

They left Granny's mansion and crossed the road to the factory.

"You must listen and learn, Barnaby," she announced. "You need to look after your mother now that your father has gone."

"My dad is coming back," said Barnaby, feeling upset at the mention of his dad's name.

"How many times do I have to tell you?" she

said. "That good-for-nothing has abandoned you."

"He is not a 'good-for-nothing' and he would never do that," shouted Barnaby, all thoughts of getting round Granny forgotten.

She stopped and glared at him. He took a step back, startled by his own outburst.

"You're obviously not ready for this," she said, and turned back towards the house.

"Wait," called Barnaby. "I'm sorry for shouting. Please, I really want to learn all about the family business."

She had to believe he was interested in her factory if he was ever going to get into that cellar. He couldn't mess it up; he had to do it for his dad.

Granny hesitated, and then walked back towards him.

"I suppose it's good to see you've got a bit of

gumption, and you're not a complete sniveller," she said. "Come on then, we mustn't be late for the flag raising."

CHAPTER 9
The Factory

They stood for a moment staring up at the letters HPC, entwined in the middle of the great iron gates which led into Hogsflesh Pickle Company.

"Why do you hate my dad so much?" Barnaby asked.

Granny Hogsflesh peered through the gates at the huge factory.

"You have to understand that I am respected in this town.

People look up to me. I'm even thinking of running for mayor next year. It doesn't look good if my family have nothing to do with pickles, and live in a shack, on a diet of pea fritters and pea soup."

"But I was happy."

"How could you be happy, boy? You didn't have any money. Besides, the fool tried to ruin. . ." She stopped suddenly.

"Ruin what?"

"Everything," she muttered. "Anyway, he's not around now, so let's get on. We've got a lot to see today."

He wanted to ask her more, but an elderly security man had approached from the gatehouse. "Good morning, Mrs *Ho-flay*."

He pronounced it just how Granny liked it. "May I say how well you're looking today?" he croaked. "And young Barnaby. How are you, young man?"

"He's fine, Mr Brown. Now stop fussing and let me into my own factory," she snapped.

Barnaby smiled apologetically at the old man before watching the gates swing open.

He had been here with his granny before, but had never taken a great interest. Now he had reason to look at everything very carefully, to see if there were any clues which could lead to his dad.

From the outside the factory looked very old-fashioned, with its red brickwork, iron gates and three enormous chimneys. However, the inside was very different. A white tiled floor in the reception area was arranged to make a huge mosaic of the company emblem – the purple initials HPC inside a white onion inside a purple egg. It was so grand that Barnaby felt he couldn't walk over it and skirted around the side.

They walked on to the vast factory floor. It was very bright. Everything was made from shiny white plastic, which gleamed under the fluorescent lights. It was dominated by a narrow spotless road, spiralling up like a giant white corkscrew, from the centre of the huge hall to a great glass box suspended from the ceiling – Granny's office. Huge vats of vinegar lined the walls, with row after row of scrubbed white tables covering the floor. Behind the tables stood the factory workers, all dressed in mauve hats, boots and overalls with a purple company emblem on the back.

Granny led Barnaby past the purple workforce up on to a white podium at one end of the hall as a hush filled the building and everyone turned to face them. Two long banners stretching from the ceiling to the floor hung behind them. One was emblazoned with an onion the size of a car, the other with an enormous egg. All the staff stood to attention as Granny turned on a microphone.

"Good morning, everyone," she bellowed.

"Good morning, Mrs *Ho-flay*." The sound of hundreds of voices echoed around the hall.

"The onion and the egg," boomed Granny, gesturing to the banners behind her. "That is how it all started. But which came first, the onion or the egg?"

There was a low murmur as the staff looked at each other, unsure how to respond.

"I will tell you." Granny paused for effect. "It doesn't matter. What matters is that our honourable onions and excellent eggs led to our glorious gherkins, champion chutneys, ravishing relishes and practically perfect piccalilli.

She was shouting now, and the crowd cheered and clapped. Granny waited for the noise to die down, nodding her approval.

"Today I have brought along my grandson, Barnaby Figg," she went on. "And I'm sure you will join me in welcoming him into the fold."

Barnaby's face burned as hundreds of people turned their attention to him. A smattering of claps soon stopped as Granny began to talk again.

"Some are born into pickles, some achieve greatness through pickles and some have pickles thrust upon them."

Barnaby was sure she glanced down at him.

"But I have a dream," she continued, her eyes blazing. "I believe that pickles are our future. Why stop at food? With our dedication and our technology, we can pickle anything we want to. We can achieve anything we want to. The world is ours to take. Nothing is unpicklable!"

The crowd roared their appreciation. Granny lapped it up, her face glistening with sweat. Barnaby didn't know how she did it. Her staff were terrified of her, and she was very rude to most of them, but she still managed to instil a passion and loyalty.

"At this very moment, *Ho-flay* scientists are developing pickles which will transform society. And with a workforce such as this. . ."

She stretched both arms out to the waiting masses. They seemed to lean towards her.

"*Ho-flay* Pickles will be national, *Ho-flay* Pickles will be global, *Ho-flay* Pickles will be universal, and you . . . you are Ho-*flay* Pickles."

The whooping and cheering drowned out Granny's voice, but she turned the microphone up and carried on.

"So stand proud and sing loud as we raise our

flag and give thanks to our beloved company. Today's flag raiser will be. . ." She waited for the crowd to calm down. Barnaby could feel an air of anticipation.

". . .Norma Mulholland."

More cheering as a small lady made her way up the steps to the podium, her face flushed with excitement.

"For her ongoing commitment towards pickling excellence."

The applause faded as the first bars of the company anthem blasted from two huge speakers. The sound of the workers' voices bounced off the walls and reverberated around the factory.

"Long live *Ho-flay* Pickle Company
We pledge undying pickle loyalty
We're so happy when we're working
Chopping onions, eggs and gherkins"

The little lady hoisted the flag with the company logo, high above the hall, as everyone sang on. The sound was deafening.

"Sing out loud and don't be silly
Celebrate our piccalilli
New York, Paris, Rome and Putney
None can beat our mango chutney"

Barnaby looked over at Granny. She was belting out the anthem, her eyes moist with emotion, the feather on her hat bobbing up and down furiously.

"Long live *Ho-flay* Pickle Company
We love you with a deep sincerity
We are faithful, we're not fickle
We are here to serve and pickle"

All faces were tilted towards the flag. Granny wiped a tear from her cheek and turned the microphone back on.

"HIP HIP," she boomed.

"*HO-FLAY*," yelled the crowd.

She did this three times and the last "*HO-FLAY*" was so rousing, Barnaby found himself joining in. A loud horn sounded and everyone turned from the flag to the tables, their faces glowing. Granny had worked them up into a pickling frenzy.

Baskets of fresh vegetables were brought out and a great chopping sound filled the hall. Barnaby looked out over the stripy sea of white and mauve. He felt quite overwhelmed.

"One day," said Granny, leading him down the steps, "if you keep up the good work, you could be the flag raiser."

"Wow, thanks," he said, before stopping abruptly. What was he saying? He didn't want to be the flag raiser. He had to keep focused on what he was trying to do.

The factory was so big that Granny had her own small car to get around in. It looked like a white plastic ball on three wheels. She called it the "Vinaigrette".

"We must put on our mauve overalls," said Granny, carefully taking off her hat and gloves. "Company policy."

They pulled the mauve coats on over their clothes and got in.

"Powered entirely by vinegar," said Granny, patting the steering wheel smugly as they set off. She was driving a bit fast and nearly knocked over an employee.

"Out of the way, you fool," she yelled, as the man dived to one side.

Barnaby checked his seat belt to make sure it was fastened properly. She had placed her hat on the dashboard and the feather kept tickling his nose.

"Pickled fuel," she continued. "It's going to be the next big thing. My scientists are working on it as we speak."

They drove around the edge of the enormous hall.

"This is the Standard Pickle Hall," yelled Granny.

She had to shout above the noise from the machinery which now filled the air. They shot past lines of tables, the people behind chopping away at various vegetables, while others loaded up the great vats of vinegar. Large signs were at the end of each row.

She screeched to a halt beside the piccalilli row. Barnaby lurched towards the windscreen, glad he had secured his seat belt.

"Come on," she shouted, bouncing out of the car like a big purple beach ball.

"How do you fancy actually making some piccalilli?"

She said it in the same way she might have asked him to drive a racing car. How could someone get so excited over chutney?

"Um . . . OK," said Barnaby, climbing down.

She stopped and looked at him closely. "You don't want to make piccalilli, do you?"

"Of course I do," he replied, trying to look excited. "I can't wait."

She sighed and climbed back into the Vinaigrette. "It's OK, Barnaby, I can see piccalilli isn't firing you up, but I know what will. Get back in the car. I'm going to take you somewhere very special."

CHAPTER 10

The Special Pickle Hall

They sped along to the end of the hall. A white brick wall spread out before them, but Granny didn't stop; she didn't even brake.

"Slow down!" shrieked Barnaby. "We're going to crash!"

The shiny bricks were almost upon them. She was mad. Barnaby screamed and covered his head with his arms, but the sickening crunch never came. They just kept on going. He opened one eye and slowly lowered his arms. They were in a tunnel.

"Optical illusion," chuckled Granny, putting

the car's headlights on. "You can only see the tunnel if you know it's there. It leads to the Special Pickle Hall."

They passed through into another huge hall that Barnaby had never been in before. It was much quieter and Granny drove a lot slower. It was divided up into separate rooms, each with a long window looking out on to the wide corridor they were driving along. All the staff here were dressed in white coats with a small purple HPC on the lapel.

"These are my scientists. They are working on pickles of the future."

"What are 'pickles of the future'?" asked Barnaby, peering into one of the windows as they slowly drove by. Science was his favourite subject at school and he was beginning to feel quite excited.

"Like I said in my speech, nothing is

unpicklable, and we are pickling and preserving things other than food. Let me show you."

They stopped outside a huge room and looked through the window. It was packed with glass jars, some as tall as houses, filled with vegetation. Barnaby could just make out a glass roof way above. He glanced up at the sign above the door.

PICKLED PLANTS

They stepped into the enormous room. It felt like a glass rainforest. Barnaby's overalls started sticking to his skin and he unzipped the front. Huge sun lamps beamed down from the high ceiling. Giant vats towered above them, each with a different species of tree inside. Barnaby spotted a couple of palm trees, some pines and even a big oak, its leaves waving in slow motion. The smell of vinegar was overwhelming. There were bushes of every size, and masses of flowers, from the tallest sunflower to a tiny snowdrop, all encased in their own liquid prison. Barnaby followed Granny through the maze of jars towards the back of the room.

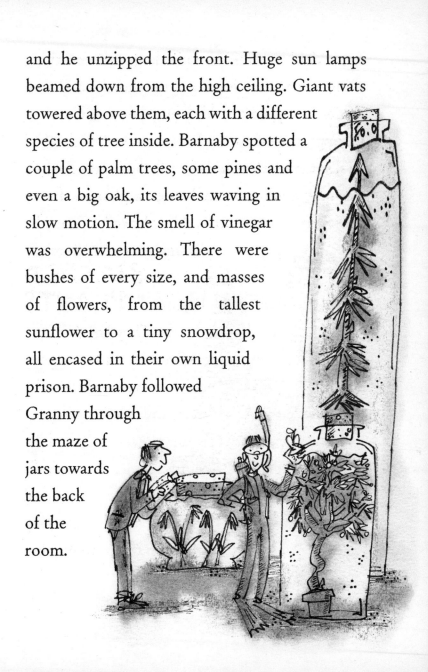

Two men holding clipboards and dressed in white coats were staring into what looked like a massive aquarium. They nodded to Granny as she approached.

"Don't mind us," said Granny. "Carry on. I'm just showing my grandson our latest developments."

Barnaby peered into the great tank. It was full of plants and flowers waving eerily in the clear vinegar. There even appeared to be a perfectly manicured lawn at the bottom.

"Soon we are hoping to create a whole pickled garden for busy people with no outdoor space," explained Granny. "We will grow the plants and then pickle them. No more dull winter gardens. It will be spring, summer or even autumn for ever, no watering or weeding needed."

Barnaby gazed inside. A scuba diver swam out from behind a pickled apple tree, making him jump. He picked an apple from the tree and gave the two men in white coats a thumbs up. One of the scientists made a note on his clipboard, while the other checked a temperature gauge.

"Come on," whispered Granny. "They are very busy and I don't want to disturb them."

They made their way outside and stood for a moment cooling down.

"What do you think?" asked Granny.

"I think it's great," said Barnaby. He was starting to enjoy himself. Granny looked very pleased.

"You could do pickled flowers for Mother's Day," he suggested. "They wouldn't wither."

"Excellent idea," beamed Granny. "You're getting a feel for this, Barnaby."

They drove along to the next section.

PICKLED RUBBISH

"Why would you want to keep your rubbish?"

asked Barnaby, pressing his face against the window to get a good look. This room looked like a city dump. The scientists inside wore protective suits and masks over their faces. They were sifting through the piles of waste, separating it into different containers.

"Soon every person in this country will have pickling bins full of vinegar outside their houses," said Granny. "Just lift the lid and pop in your leftovers. The bin men won't have to come for weeks on end. It will save the councils a fortune."

"What about the rest of your rubbish?" asked Barnaby, watching the men put plastic bags and bottles into a separate container.

Granny frowned. "That's a problem we're working on at the moment. Maybe one day, you will come up with an answer, Barnaby."

They drove on slowly, stopping at each department. Barnaby hated to admit it, but he was having fun.

"You said that you could pickle anything," he said.

"And I meant it," said Granny. "But if you come up with a new idea, come to me first. You can't trust anyone round here. Not long ago I had the brilliant idea of displaying my pickles as great works of art. One of my scientists ran off with the idea. Last I heard he was pickling sharks, cows and zebras, and doing very well for himself."

Granny sniffed angrily and pulled up outside the next long window.

"Take a look in here," she said, brightening up. "This one is going to make us a lot of money."

This room was a lot smaller and calmer than the previous one. Relaxing music was being piped in, and rows of beautifully shaped jars filled the shelves. The scientists inside looked much younger compared with the others he had seen. One of them looked up at Barnaby and smiled. He grinned back and checked the sign above.

PICKLED FACE CREAM

"We're still in the early stages of development with this one," said Granny. "But eventually, if they use our formula from a young age, everyone will be able to preserve their youthful skin. We can't use vinegar as it distorts the colour of the skin, but we have been experimenting with special oils instead, and look at the results."

She gestured at the fresh-faced scientists.

"I wonder if we could develop something for hair and teeth too?" asked Barnaby.

"Nothing is impossible," said Granny. "And I think we are going to make a great team."

Granny's last comment stopped Barnaby in his tracks. For a moment he had forgotten about his dad.

At last they came to the final room. Three men in white coats were gathered round a glass bowl. One of them looked up and saw Granny Hogsflesh. She pointed to the glass bowl and beckoned the man over. He came closer and held it up to the window. It was a goldfish floating in the water.

"Why isn't it swimming?" asked Barnaby.

"Because it died two weeks ago," said Granny, proudly. "It died from old age, and what do people do with their goldfish when they die?"

"I don't know," he said. "I suppose they flush them down the toilet or bury them."

"Exactly, and they never see them again. Well, now you can pickle them and look at them for ever."

She let out a loud burp in her excitement and Barnaby turned away. It was then that he noticed the sign on the door.

PICKLED PETS

"And this is just the beginning," continued Granny, eagerly. "Soon we will be able to pickle budgies, gerbils, even dogs."

She gave the scientist a nod and he returned to his colleagues.

"You keep talking about getting a dog," she said, getting back into the Vinaigrette. "I'll get you a pickled one – how about that?"

"That's very kind, Granny," said Barnaby,

climbing in beside her, "but I think I would rather have a live one."

She looked a little disappointed.

"I can't believe you pickle pets," he said. He didn't like the last department.

"I can pickle anything I want to," said Granny, huffily. "All you need is a bit of research and a few experiments. I could pickle you if I wanted."

The words "experimental pickling" leapt into his head. Granny leaned towards him. A stale vinegary smell drifted up his nose as she put her lumpy lips close to his ear and whispered, "If you can pickle pets, then why not people?"

This was too much. A wave of revulsion swamped him as he realized that Granny was capable of anything. He tried to keep his breathing even.

"When can we visit the cellar?" he asked, trying to force the words "pickled people" out of his mind.

She leaned back and studied his face closely.

"Still very interested in my cellar, aren't we?" she said.

"It's just that now I've seen all this," he replied, "I can't wait to learn more."

This seemed to satisfy her.

"You've done very well today, Barnaby, but I think that's enough for one day. You go back to the house now and tomorrow you can work in my office."

CHAPTER 11
The Curse

Barnaby felt shaken as he left the factory. Was Granny seriously thinking about pickling people? What would be the point of that? She was obviously trying to scare him, or just show off her pickling prowess. He crossed the road and walked through the huge front doors of the enormous house. All was quiet. The cleaner had gone, the cook wasn't due in yet, his mum was at the pea farm and Granny was still at the factory. He was all alone.

Barnaby made his way to the stone staircase that led down to the cellar. What was she hiding down there? There was no dim light at the bottom as there had been before. He stared into the thick blackness below. If he could just find the courage to get down the steps, open the door and peek inside, then he could find out. He had managed to do it before. He put his hands against the cold, damp wall, closed his eyes and started the descent. Eventually he felt his way to the bottom. His hands touched the old oak door, but it didn't feel old or oak. It was smooth like metal. He couldn't find the key and opened his eyes for a moment but shut them again, afraid of the complete darkness. He pressed his ear against the door and listened.

"Dad?" he called tentatively.

The silence wrapped around him.

"Dad, are you in there?"

He started banging on the door with his fists.

"DAD," he yelled, "DAD, CAN YOU HEAR ME?"

He stood for a moment in the stillness, feeling foolish. Cautiously he climbed back up the staircase, not opening his eyes until he reached the top. He felt completely drained. It had been a long day. Maybe he didn't want to see inside the cellar without Granny. Who knew what was in there.

Barnaby went back to his room. Tomorrow he was working in Granny's office, and if he got a chance he might be able to look up bogles on her computer. But the one thing he could do right now was to read the diary. He hadn't had a chance to look at it since yesterday. It was a while until dinner and Barnaby needed to find out what happened to poor Mary Morley. The last thing he had read about her had been awful. She had accidentally taken a baby and been cursed by its mother. He took the little diary out of his pocket and fell back on to his bed.

January 7th

I thought yesterday was bad, but today has been even worse. I'm beginning to understand what the curse of the bogle's beard is about. Mother explained to me that bogles live under the peat bogs in the forest near our farm. They are so rarely seen by humans that not many people believe they are real. But Mother knew all about them. She explained how they hate humans and only come above ground to cause trouble.

This morning I had a very itchy face. At breakfast, mother reached across the table and plucked a long black hair from my chin. I immediately burped right in her face - felt awful. Then later, in the pickling shed, I was horrified to see that I had unintentionally chopped up the beetroot into very rude shapes. Rows of beetroot bottoms stared up at me. I couldn't believe it and hacked them into tiny pieces, threw them into the jars of vinegar and went to Mrs Cave-Brown-Cave's house to deliver her order.

Barnaby stopped reading and smiled at the thought of the beetroot bottoms. However, the hairy chin and uncontrollable rudeness all sounded very familiar. It was exactly what had happened to Dad. What if a bogle had visited his dad at the farm? He could have been cursed, just like poor Mary. But why would a bogle do that to him?

January 8th

I woke up this morning with more long black hairs on my chin. Pulled most of them out but they are growing faster than I can pluck. Just after breakfast a furious Mrs Cave-Brown-Cave turned up on our doorstep. She slammed a large jar of beetroot down on the table and told my mother and father how she had sat down to breakfast this morning, opened the lid of beetroot and was faced with a small purple pickled bottom.

My parents tried to calm her down but she cancelled her orders with us and stormed out. Mother says we are ruined. Father says the first thing we must do is break the curse. I have to go into the forest and find the bogle village. I must track down the bogle mother and seek her forgiveness. My parents have given me a present to give to her. It's the only thing we have - a beetroot.

Barnaby would have liked to carry on reading, but it was dinner time and Granny wouldn't like it if he was late. He was the first down to the dining room and sat at the long table, waiting. He missed his mum's pea soup and pea fritters. They didn't have peas at all any more because Granny didn't like them. Mum came hurrying in and gave him a big hug.

"How was your day?" she asked, anxiously.

"Strange," he said. "I found out all about pickled pets amongst other things."

"Yes, I've heard about that," said Mum, pulling a face.

"But," he said, looking over his shoulder to make sure they were still alone, "I think I may have found out what was wrong with Dad. I think he was cursed by a bogle – the curse of the bogle's beard."

Mum frowned and crouched down beside him.

"Yesterday, you said Dad had been locked away by Granny," she said, "and today you say he's been cursed by a bogle. What will it be tomorrow, Barnaby? Abducted by aliens?"

Barnaby sighed. Now was the time to tell her about the diary. But what if she showed it to Granny and he never got to finish it? He had to read it first and then show it to her.

"Did you find out what Granny's parents were called?" he asked.

"Not yet," she said, "but I did look up 'bogle' in the dictionary. It's a fictional creature, like a goblin. Do you know what fictional means, Barnaby?"

"Made up," he said, grudgingly.

"That's right. The woman who visited the pea farm was just a small and unfortunate-looking person."

"Well, who was this 'small and unfortunate-looking person', then?"

"I don't know," said Mum. "Maybe she just wanted to buy some peas. But I do know that she was not a bogle!"

They both jumped as the dining room doors slammed behind them. They looked round to see Granny Hogsflesh standing there, her face like thunder.

"Who mentioned bogles?" she yelled.

"It was me, Mother," said Mum. "I was just explaining to Barnaby that there is—"

"How could you fill the boy's head with such rubbish?" she shouted.

"I wasn't, I was just—"

"There are no such things as bogles," cried Granny. "And I never want them mentioned again."

"But when I was a little girl, you used to blame everything on 'the bogles'," said Mum.

Granny winced. "I don't care what I used to do," she snapped. "That was before I was a somebody. But now I have a reputation to maintain, and I don't want that sort of trivial nonsense being bandied around my house. Do you both understand?"

Not yet, thought Barnaby, nodding at his granny, *but it won't be long before I do.*

CHAPTER 12
The Office

Barnaby woke up early the next day. He lay in bed thinking about the previous night. Dinner had been very strained and nobody had talked. When Mum had come in to say goodnight, she said she couldn't understand Granny's outburst. Why were they not allowed to mention bogles? Mum put it down to superstition and old age, but there was some doubt in her voice. Barnaby hoped she was beginning to suspect that he wasn't the only one who thought bogles might be real.

At breakfast, Granny seemed to have completely recovered and was excited about taking Barnaby into her office at the factory. She wasn't quite as rude to the poor gate man, choosing to ignore rather than insult him. After singing the company anthem, they jumped in the Vinaigrette.

"Because we are not working on the factory floor today," she said, "we won't need to put our overalls on."

Granny drove like a maniac up the white corkscrew path that led to the glass office suspended from the ceiling. She managed to knock over a couple of employees on the way.

"Idiots," she yelled behind her, as the poor people staggered off.

The office was divided into two sections. The first one was small, with rows of brightly coloured relishes and chutneys lining the glass shelves of one of the walls. Two efficient-looking ladies sat in front of computers. They got up as Granny entered.

"Good morning, Mrs *Ho-flay*," they said in unison.

"Good morning, Grace, good morning . . . um . . . other one," Granny said, walking straight past and throwing her coat at the "other one". "Barnaby will be working with us today."

He said good morning and smiled politely at them as he walked through into the second, much bigger room. Granny closed the door behind them and opened her arms wide.

"This is it, Barnaby," she said, "the nerve centre of *Ho-flay* Pickles. What do you think?"

It was quite spectacular, if a little scary. You could look through the glass floor at all the workers below in the Standard Pickle Hall.

"I can always keep an eye on that lot from up here. And if I need a little privacy?" She pressed a button and all the glass turned purple.

"Wow!" said Barnaby. He wanted to have a go but was afraid to ask.

She pressed the button again and the glass returned to normal.

Granny sat down at her long desk. The wall behind her was covered in glass shelves filled with jars. Barnaby peered into them, expecting to find more chutneys, but was shocked to discover they were filled with pickled insects. Spiders, flies, beetles, cockroaches, maggots, worms and things he had never seen before covered the entire wall. At least it wasn't as bad as pickled pets.

"Ah, I see you like my little collection," she said.

"What do you use pickled insects for?" he asked, screwing up his nose.

"I don't use them for anything. I just think they brighten the place up, don't you?"

Barnaby picked up a jar and studied the gruesome bug inside. It was bright green with dangly hairy legs. A narrow neck led to an elongated head, out of which grew a long vicious snout.

"I see you've chosen my favourite one," said Granny, taking the jar from him. "The assassin bug. Isn't he a beauty? He stabs his feeding tube into his prey and injects them with a lethal poison before sucking out their insides."

Barnaby grimaced.

"Like a spider," he said.

"Oh no, assassin bugs are much more intelligent than spiders," she went on, her eyes glowing. "Assassins don't just hang around waiting for their prey to come to them, they set a trap – they lure them in."

Granny seemed totally entranced by the insect. She was dribbling with enthusiasm. Barnaby took a step back.

"They pluck spiders' webs, fooling them into thinking they have caught something, and then once within reach they lunge, stabbing the foolish arachnid with their lethal proboscis."

Barnaby stared at her, not knowing what to say.

"Like I said, brightens the place up," she grinned. "But now we need to get down to some work."

Granny put the assassin bug back on to the shelf and returned to her desk.

"My recipes are top secret, so I keep them all right here in my office. I've been looking at relishes and chutneys from around the world and I need you to file them away for me."

She handed him a tall pile of recipe sheets and led him to a locked cabinet in the corner of the room. The day passed slowly and Barnaby felt very frustrated. He hadn't found out anything, except for Granny's love of violent insects. He had to ask her some awkward questions without her becoming suspicious. He took a deep breath, closed the filing cabinet and turned to his grandmother.

"Granny?" asked Barnaby. "What was Grandpa Hogsflesh like?"

She looked up over her computer.

"What do you want to know about him for?" she asked.

"Just because he was my grandpa and I didn't know him."

Granny got up and locked the drawer containing all the recipes.

"Always smelled of onions," she said, walking back to the computer.

"Is that it?" asked Barnaby, disappointed.

"Well, what do you want to know, boy? Can't you see I'm busy?"

"I just want to know a little bit more."

"OK, but I have to be quick. They need me down in Special Pickles," she said, packing up her desk. "We met when we were both eighteen, got married, started to pickle the onions on his farm and the eggs from my chickens, sold lots, had your mother, sold more, started the factory, got rich, he died, you were born, here we are." She got up to go. "OK?"

"Were your farms close?" asked Barnaby.

"Yes," she said, "next door."

"Did Grandpa grow up on his farm?"

"Yes. Now I really have to go." She pulled on her purple boots.

"If you both grew up on next-door farms, how come you only met when you were eighteen?" he asked.

Granny Hogsflesh had her back to Barnaby. She stopped for a moment, then continued putting on her overalls.

"You ask too many questions, Barnaby, and like I said, I have to go."

Barnaby could tell that she wasn't pleased and he had to stay in her good books.

"While you're away this afternoon, can I do some research on the computer into Indian and Japanese pickles?" he asked. "I saw some recipes when I was doing the filing and thought they looked really interesting."

A broad smile spread across Granny's face.

"Barnaby Figg," she said, "I do believe that you are turning into the grandson I always wanted." Barnaby felt a little guilty. He didn't like deceiving anyone, but Granny was beginning to trust him and he had to play on that.

"I'll be about an hour or so. Ask Grace or what's-her-name if you need anything."

When Granny left, Barnaby sat at her computer

thinking about his grandpa. His mum thought they had grown up together, but Granny said they hadn't met until she was eighteen. So where had she been before that? Did she grow up on the farm or somewhere else?

Barnaby turned on the computer. He had a quick look at an "Eastern Pickles" website in case Granny asked him about it later and he jotted down some notes, and then he typed in "BOGLES".

BOGLES

THE TERM "BOGLE" COMES FROM THE WORD GOBLIN. BOGLES HAVE FIERCE TEMPERS AND CAN SOMETIMES BE DANGEROUS. THEY LOVE TO ANNOY HUMAN BEINGS. THEY CAN MAKE HUMANS HEAR VOICES ROUND CORNERS WHEN NO ONE IS THERE. THEY ENTER HOUSES AND MAKE A MESS OR CAUSE THINGS TO HAPPEN AT THE WRONG TIME.

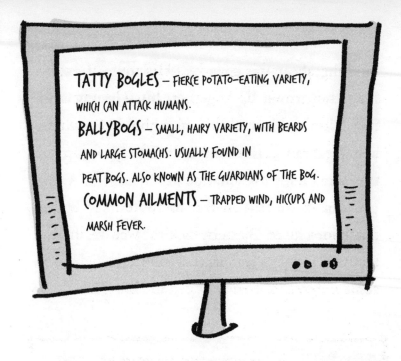

TATTY BOGLES – FIERCE POTATO-EATING VARIETY, WHICH CAN ATTACK HUMANS.

BALLYBOGS – SMALL, HAIRY VARIETY, WITH BEARDS AND LARGE STOMACHS. USUALLY FOUND IN PEAT BOGS. ALSO KNOWN AS THE GUARDIANS OF THE BOG.

COMMON AILMENTS – TRAPPED WIND, HICCUPS AND MARSH FEVER.

Barnaby checked several other websites and noted down all the information he could find. Messy rooms, strange voices – all the information was pointing towards bogles in Granny's house. But was it the same bogle that had visited his dad? And why did it visit Granny?

He was so caught up in his thoughts, he didn't realize how long his research had taken and he didn't hear the click of the door as Granny Hogsflesh came back in. The first he knew of it was a wrinkly hand on his shoulder. She was peering down at the computer. The whole screen was filled with information about bogles. A low growling sound escaped from her pursed lips as she bent closer. Barnaby couldn't move. It was too late to delete the page.

CHAPTER 13
What Father?

Barnaby held his breath. Granny looked at the screen through narrowed eyes and shook her head angrily.

"I can't see a thing without my glasses," she said, bending down to get them out of her bag. Quick as a flash Barnaby clicked the little cross in the corner of the screen and the page disappeared to reveal a website underneath with the heading: **TSUKEMONO – THE JAPANESE VARIETY OF PICKLE.**

"This looks interesting, Barnaby," she said, popping back up.

"Oh, it is, Granny, and I was also surprised to

find that Indian pickles can be preserved in oil."

"That's right," she grinned. "You are a fast learner."

Granny bent down so that her face was right beside his. They were both staring straight ahead at the computer. *Please don't turn towards me,* thought Barnaby. But she did. She was so close that her long nose was tickling his cheek.

"I was wrong about you, Barnaby," she said. "I thought you were as dim-witted as your father."

Barnaby tensed up, but managed to recover. He mustn't let her see how he felt; this was the chance he had been waiting for. He steeled himself and turned to face her. Their noses were almost touching and he flinched slightly as he caught a waft of her musty breath.

"You were right about him," he said. "He's not coming back and I need to forget about him."

Granny slowly got up and stood behind Barnaby, resting her hands on his shoulders.

"At last," she said. "You have finally come to your senses."

He could see her face reflected in the computer screen. She was smiling.

"I belong here in the factory with you," he continued. "The family business is the most important thing and I need to learn everything there is to know."

The fingers on his shoulders tightened.

"Your father might not approve," she said, slyly.

Barnaby's heart was hammering, but he had to hold his nerve.

"What father?" he said.

Granny snorted triumphantly and walked round the desk to face him, her saggy jowls wobbling excitedly.

"Does this mean I can trust you now, Barnaby?" she whispered.

"Yes, Granny," he said, trying to keep an even voice. "You can trust me with anything."

"Not just *anything*," she breathed. "But with the secrets of *Ho-flay* Pickles."

He knew it. She was hiding something.

"I am here to serve and pickle," he said solemnly.

"Then it is time," she whispered. "Time for you to see in the cellar, time for you to learn about . . . the dark side of pickling."

CHAPTER 14
The Bog

"Granny's taking me down to the cellar tomorrow," said Barnaby to his mum that night. It was late and he was sitting up in bed.

She raised an eyebrow. "What are you up to?" she asked.

"*I'm* not up to anything," he said. "*She* is, and I'm going to find out what. She's hiding something down there, and that's not all. She didn't grow up with Grandpa like she told you. She didn't even meet him until she was eighteen. So she's lying about something."

"I'm not sure I like where this is leading,"

said Mum.

"You want to find Dad, don't you?" he asked.

"Of course I do, but what has any of this got to do with your dad?"

Barnaby hesitated. He still wasn't ready to tell her about the diary. "Dad was visited by that odd little woman just before he started growing that horrible beard and acting strangely," he said. "Mr Pottage said she looked like a hairy beetroot."

"Oh, not this again," said Mum, getting up to go.

Barnaby grabbed her arm. "Just hear me out – please, Mum?"

She paused for a moment, then sat back down on the bed.

"Go on," she sighed.

"I looked up bogles on Granny's computer." Barnaby got out his notes. "There is a small, hairy variety, with beards and large stomachs.

They love to annoy humans and can make people hear voices round corners when no one is there. They can enter houses and make a mess or cause things to happen at the wrong time."

"OK," said Mum, "but they're still not real."

"There are strange things going on in this house," continued Barnaby. "Wrecked rooms, footsteps but no one there, voices but no one there."

Mum looked slightly shaken.

"You've heard them too," he said accusingly.

"It's an old house," she said. "Things creak."

But Barnaby could hear the uncertainty in her voice.

"Dad was visited by a bogle just before he went missing," he said, "and this house is visited by bogles, and Granny won't have the word mentioned in her house. You saw her reaction. There has to be a connection."

Mum fiddled with the embossed egg on his pillowcase. Barnaby felt pleased he had at last planted a seed of suspicion in her mind.

"This is all getting very weird," she said.

"That's because Granny's very weird. Where was she for the first eighteen years of her life? Who were her parents? Surely you want to know too."

Mum stopped fiddling with the pillowcase and plumped it up for Barnaby to lie down.

"All right, I'll think about it," she said. "I know where she keeps all her personal documents. Her birth certificate will have the full names of her parents on it. But if nothing comes of this and Dad doesn't contact us soon, then I'm going to report him as a missing person."

"OK, thanks, Mum. See you in the morning."

"Goodnight, Barnaby."

As soon as she closed the door, Barnaby got out the diary. He had to find out if Mary Morley had managed to find the bogle mother and break the curse of the bogle's beard.

January 9th
It is dark and it is cold. I am sitting here under a tree wrapped in a blanket with only a beetroot for company. I wandered for miles today trying to find signs of bogles, but nothing. I'm so glad I brought my diary with me. It is comforting to write in.

January 10th
Still nothing. My food supply is running out. I will have to return home tomorrow if I cannot find the bogles. I am not looking forward to another night in the forest. I'm cold and hungry.

January 11th

Today I started the long journey home. I was very tired and glad to see the familiar sight of the bogs and fens that are close to our farm. I started to run but tripped on a root and fell right into the bog. It started sucking me in. I was certain I would be pulled under and killed. I managed to grab hold of a tree root and cling on but my hand slipped down and I was pulled in up to my waist. I screamed as I lost my grip and suddenly I was up to my chin in cold, wet bog. I took a last gulp of breath and held it as my mouth and nose went in. But the minute my head went under, a strange bubble formed around it and I could breathe. My relief turned to panic as I was sucked down faster. I shot out into open air and landed on a bed of moss with a great thump. High above me was a ceiling of mud and stone, the roots of trees poking down, and there was the most dreadful dank, boggy smell. I realized that I had landed in the middle of a village square, in a huge underground cavern. Burning lamps lit up winding gravel paths, lined with completely round houses made of mud. Most were made up of two or three balls of mud joined together. But the thing which filled me with excitement and terror were the creatures climbing in and out of these strange buildings - bogles.

Barnaby sat up in bed. He couldn't quite believe what he was reading. It crossed his mind that the diary could all be a lie. What if Mary Morley's life on the beetroot farm was so dull, she made up the whole thing just to make her diary more interesting? He glanced at his watch. It was nearly eleven o'clock and he was getting very sleepy. But the entry for January 11th was a long one and he had to finish it.

I couldn't believe my luck. After giving up hope of finding it I had literally stumbled into the bogle village. I walked around the square of mud houses, my heart thumping. The first bogle to spot me stared with astonishment and then anger. He burped loudly, then cried, "A human!" Others stopped what they were doing and looked around. More came out of their round mud huts. "A human, a human." I could hear the words going from bogle to bogle. They crowded round me until I was surrounded. It seemed like the whole village was glaring at me. What strange creatures, like small fat children with beards. It was very hard to tell the men from the women. I fitted in quite well with my hairy chin.

I wasn't sure what to do next but then a large bogle, nearly as tall as me, stepped forward. I couldn't tell where his hair ended and his beard began. It was like a lion's mane and he looked just as fierce. He told the others he would deal with me and they started to drift away. I told him my name, but he knew who I was. He said his name was Baldric Ballybog and I followed him along a narrow winding path to the biggest house in the village. It had at least five mud balls attached to the first larger one and was set back from the other houses. He pushed me through the door. It was dark inside and it took a while to see properly. There standing

in front of me was the bogle mother who
had cursed me. "This is my sister," he said,
"Burpina Ballybog."

Burpina ran to a cot when she saw me and
picked up the wrinkled baby that I had found
on our farm. It immediately started burping.
"My poor little Belchetta," she cooed, rubbing
the child's back. I tried to explain that I had
been searching for her for days and had
come to apologize, but Burpina would not
listen and told me to get out.

I said I thought the baby had been left
and begged for her forgiveness. I told her
I had brought a present to say how sorry
I was, and put my beetroot on the table.
They stared at it and I thought I saw Baldric
Ballybog start to smile, but Burpina let out a
furious belch.

"You think a beetroot will make up for

stealing my child?" she yelled. She said I wasn't sorry at all and just wanted to break the curse of the bogle's beard. Then she threw the beetroot at me and left the room, taking her squealing baby with her.

I went back through the front door on to the path outside. Baldric Ballybog led me through the maze of houses to the bottom of a narrow ladder that reached up to the top of the cavern to a tree root poking out of the ceiling. He told me that I could never break the curse, as I had to be kissed by a bogle, which would never happen. Then with a farewell belch, he pointed to the ladder and told me to climb.

The ladder was enormous, but eventually I reached the root and hauled myself up inside a hollow tree. I could see daylight coming through a gap at the top. I squeezed through the hole and dropped down on to the forest floor, panting for breath, glad of the fresh air.

I don't know what to do next, but I cannot give up. I cannot live with the curse of the bogle's beard. I have to think of something.

Barnaby heard footsteps outside and closed the diary. It was very late and everyone was in bed. He waited, straining his ears to hear more. Someone was outside his door. Wasn't that what bogles loved to do, enter houses and make humans hear noises?

The onion doorknob slowly turned and Barnaby held his breath. It stopped. Silence. He crept out of bed. If he actually saw a bogle, then he would know Mary was telling the truth. He could still hear shuffling from the other side and flung it open. But the landing was completely empty. He searched the hall in frustration – nothing. Eventually he flopped back on to the bed. He felt sure there were bogles in this house, but why? What did they want with his family? Perhaps he would find out more in the cellar.

CHAPTER 15
The Cellar

"I'm not pea picking today," said Mum at breakfast. "I've got the day off and thought I could spend it with Barnaby."

"Well, you can't," said Granny Hogsflesh, pieces of pickled shrimp flying out of her mouth. "He's working with me today . . . in the cellar."

She gave Barnaby a spongy, wet smile. He managed to smile back although his stomach was churning.

"Is that what you really want to do, Barnaby?" asked Mum.

"Yes," he said firmly.

She gave him a slight nod of the head.

"Why don't you read up on pickles in the library, Hatty?" said Granny. "Barnaby did, and now he's taken a real interest. Let's forget about peas, now *that man* is out of the way. Let's make pickling a real family business again."

"That man..." began Mum furiously. Barnaby kicked her gently under the table and she stopped, but he could see she was still mad. She got up to go. "I have other things to get on with today, Mother," she said, marching through the doors. "I'll see you tonight, Barnaby."

Granny swallowed the last bit of her briny breakfast.

"Ready, young man?" she asked.

"Yes I am," he said, trying to look calm.

"Let's go, then. Hurry up and finish your pickled cabbage; it boosts your immune system, and you're going to need it."

Granny led Barnaby to the spiralling stone steps. An icy draught blew up his trousers.

"Cold, isn't it?" she said.

He nodded, but it wasn't the wind that was making him shiver.

"There are no workers in here," said Granny, slowly making her way down the steps. "I do all the dark pickling myself, but I am getting old and I need help. Watch, listen and . . . Barnaby? Where are you?"

He was still at the top.

"I'm coming," he called. He couldn't lose his nerve now. He tried to keep his knees under control as he made his way down. At least it wasn't pitch-black now. The dull lamp below was switched on, lighting up Granny and the huge oak door. She reached for the large key in the lock that he had noticed before, but couldn't find on his last visit.

"You see this key?" she said. "If anyone tries to turn it, alarm bells go off and I know there is an intruder."

Thank goodness he hadn't tried it last time. She pulled the key out of the door and pushed it into a hole in the side of the lamp beside them. A control panel slowly dropped from the lamp. She typed in the number 666.

"My lucky number," she said.

Barnaby realized that the old oak door wasn't old

or oak, just as he had suspected, but a high-tech metal which slowly slid down into the floor, revealing a second metal door with what looked like a pair of binoculars sticking out from it.

"Look into them, Barnaby; I need to scan your eyes. You and I will be the only ones allowed access. The dark pickling must be kept within the family and I can't manage it on my own any more. That is why I need you by my side."

Barnaby pressed his eyes to the holes. It was completely black, and then a red line passed from the top of the screen to the bottom and from left to right. There was a ping like a microwave finishing.

"All done," said Granny. "Every person's eyes are different, like fingerprints. The computer scans our eyes and identifies a person before opening the door. There is top secret work in here. No one else is allowed in."

She pushed a silver button beneath the eye scanners.

"Unfortunately it doesn't work on everything," she muttered.

The metal door slid up into the ceiling above. Barnaby shivered and stepped in.

They entered a long, dark room. The walls and ceilings were curved round like a tunnel. It was dimly lit and very cold.

"Low lighting and temperature are essential in dark pickling," said Granny. "But we'll go into that later. First, you must understand what we are doing here."

They made their way in, Barnaby checking around for any evidence that his dad may have been here. Eight cave-like rooms led off from the main area, four on either side. There were wooden signs above the arched openings, and vats the size of a man, each with a small ladder attached, lined the centre of the room.

"These are big," he said, pointing to one of the vats. "Big enough to fit a whole person in."

He watched her reaction closely.

"Maybe even two," said Granny.

The hairs on the back of Barnaby's neck pricked up.

"Are they full of vinegar?" he asked, trying to keep his voice steady.

"Not just vinegar. Dark pickles are much more complicated than that."

Barnaby tried to swallow, but his mouth was so dry, there was nothing there. He had a question to ask and he wasn't sure he wanted to know the answer.

"What exactly are dark pickles?"

"Ahh," said Granny, stopping before they reached the first entrance. "Dark pickles are made for international clients. Their identities must be kept top secret. They are specialists in their fields."

"What fields?" asked Barnaby, peering into the gloom of the first room. A table stood in the middle with rows of glass jars crammed on to the shelves all around.

"We must never ask our clients too many questions, Barnaby. Just know that preserving foul and horrid things is a very powerful and potent business."

Barnaby stopped at the first huge vat and read the sign above the archway.

toenails

CHAPTER 16

The Dark Side of Pickling

"Who in their right mind would buy a pickled toenail?" Barnaby cried, disgusted.

"Very popular in muggy climates," said Granny Hogsflesh. "Witch doctors love them. But you must be extremely careful when handling them. A single prick from certain kinds can be deadly."

"Witch doctors? Some of your clients are witch doctors . . . but don't they use black magic?"

"Some do," said Granny, "but most of them are healers, mixing medicine with magic."

"OK," said Barnaby, feeling slightly relieved.

"But I don't know any like that," she continued.

They moved on to the next two sections. MUCUS and Earwax.

"This is disgusting," said Barnaby. His fingers and toes were beginning to feel numb. He wasn't sure whether it was cold or shock.

"Actually, mucus and earwax are very interesting," said Granny, enthusiastically. "Earwax pickled at the correct temperature with a dash of mucus can make you feel younger and increase your strength."

"How?"

"I'm not a witch," said Granny, picking up a jar from the mucus section. "I just provide ingredients and, like I said, we never ask our clients too many questions."

She handed Barnaby the jar. Floating inside was a large green glob of goo. The label underneath read Gorilla Bogey.

"How on earth did you get a gorilla bogey?" he asked in amazement.

"It's not easy," Granny said, taking the jar and holding it up to the light. "But I have contacts at the local zoo. This little gem will make us thousands of pounds. The American market is crying out for them, and unless you are overly familiar with a gorilla, then I am the only provider."

"What are they used for?" asked Barnaby.

"I believe they are essential in vomiting potions," she said, "amongst other things."

Barnaby immediately felt sick. "Eeughh! Why would anyone want to make a vomiting potion?"

Granny frowned. "I don't know," she said. "Do I look like a witch?"

Barnaby stared at the long bent nose, stabbed into the folds of her face. Veins and wrinkles criss-crossed over bulbous lips and out across her bristly mountainous chins.

"Um. . ."

"Obviously not," she said, unaware of Barnaby's hesitation. "Like I said, I just provide the ingredients. All I know is, the stronger the beast, the stronger the bogey."

She carefully placed the jar back on the shelf.

The next two vats were bubbling madly. The smell from them was awful. Barnaby held his nose and read the signs above.

Animal gases

"I cannot believe you can pickle trumps," he said. "There must be a law against that."

"Well, you had better start believing, because these are our best-sellers," she said, pointedly ignoring the last part of his comment. "One whiff of a tarantula trump can turn a man crazy."

"Tarantulas don't trump," said Barnaby, disbelievingly.

"Oh yes they do. It's catching it that's the trick."

"And how do you do that?"

"All in good time, Barnaby, all in good time," she said, walking on towards the last three rooms.

He read the next sign still holding his nose

Verrucas

Barnaby couldn't look into the jars. Just the

thought of a pickled verruca made him feel sick.

"I don't even want to ask you about that," he said. "That is gross."

"Gross it may be, but it's also very well paid. How do you think I can afford a house like this? Not by selling pickled onions, that's for sure," said Granny.

Barnaby started to shiver and wrapped his arms around his body. They had nearly reached the end of the room, much to his relief.

"This is my experimental room," announced Granny. "Clients are always asking for new ingredients and I have to try things out. For example, teeth don't preserve very well at all, but eyeballs pickle beautifully."

She gave him another jar with two white balls bobbing in the liquid. Barnaby nearly dropped it as he realized what they were. He had now lost all feeling in his fingers and handed it back to Granny quickly.

"What sort of eyeballs are they?" he managed to say.

"They're hum—" she began, but stopped when she saw the fear in his eyes.

"They're humongous, don't you think?" she said, studying his face closely.

They didn't look particularly big to Barnaby. He was sure she was going to say "human", then changed her mind.

"I suppose," he muttered. What if Granny had pickled his dad, bit by bit?

"Are you OK, Barnaby?" she asked, still looking closely into his face.

He had to pull himself together. He was finally in the cellar and he had to carry on.

"Yes, I'm fine," he said, wiping a trickle of cold sweat from his forehead. "What's in the final area?"

"Well," said Granny, turning to the last room. "This may surprise you."

Barnaby didn't think he could handle any more surprises. He was almost afraid to read the sign.

CHAPTER 17
Black Magic

Beetroot

"Beetroot," Barnaby said, feeling very relieved. "I thought you didn't do beetroot? And why is it in dark pickling?"

"I don't recommend it as a food – nasty, horrible stuff. But as a potion. . ." She held a jar of pickled beetroot up to Barnaby's face. "Never underestimate the power of a beetroot," she whispered.

"Are all these ingredients used in black magic?" he asked.

"Well, they're not used in fairy cakes," said

Granny. "It's called dark pickling, not pink and fluffy pickling."

"It's just . . . don't you feel a bit guilty about what they may be used for?"

"We're not hurting anyone. We're just providing a service for our clients," she replied. "And some of our clients are very grateful. Look at this."

She produced a tiny silver flask from a shelf in the beetroot section. "This is a present from a very powerful medicine man – a universal antidote."

"What's an antidote?" asked Barnaby.

"It's a cure. This can work against ninety per cent of poisons."

She held it up for Barnaby to see.

"Why don't our doctors have it, then?" he asked.

"Normal medicine is all about science," she answered, going back into the beetroot cave with the silver flask. "This, however, is all about science combined with sorcery."

He lost sight of her but could hear her moving jars around.

"And think of the money," she shouted above the sound of the clinking glass.

Barnaby looked at the huge vat of vinegar beside the experimental pickling cave. Something was floating inside, thudding against the side every now and then. He wanted to take a closer look and started to climb the ladder attached to it.

"You could have your own house," Granny continued, shouting from round the corner. "All the things you ever wanted – all the things your father never gave you."

She came out and spotted Barnaby at the top of the vat looking in.

"GET DOWN, YOU STUPID BOY," she

screeched. "YOU COULD BE KILLED."

But Barnaby was rooted to the top of the ladder. Floating in the murky vinegar were several large bones.

"NOW!" yelled Granny.

He dropped down quickly.

"I told you that was not just vinegar in there. There are dark ingredients too. If you fell in you would be pickled in an instant, and that would be the end of you."

She sat down on a bench by one of the tables, breathing heavily.

Barnaby stood at the bottom of the ladder. He was scared, but now he was angry too.

"Is that what happened to the last person who fell in?" he asked.

Granny recovered slightly and sat back, looking at him. "What are you talking about?"

"There are bones in there!" he cried. He could

feel the panic rising. "You've pickled someone, admit it."

"Those are baboon bones, you stupid boy," she said, getting up and moving towards him.

"It's my dad!" he shouted. "You've pickled my dad."

Granny stopped in her tracks, the folds of her neck rippling as she swallowed hard.

CHAPTER 18
The Roman Folklore

Barnaby backed off towards the door as Granny began edging closer, her eyes darting from Barnaby to the big vat of bones.

"I know it's very easy to mistake your dad for a baboon," she said, "but why would I want to pickle that great ape?"

"Don't talk about my dad like that. I'm getting out of here," he shouted, glancing behind him. He was nearly at the entrance.

"Don't be silly, Barnaby. Don't give this all up!" cried Granny. "Join me; together we can rule the pickling empire."

"Never!" he cried, turning and running for the door. He could hear her shuffling behind him, but he was too fast. She would never catch him.

"Go, then," she yelled. "I thought you were different, but you're weak, just like that idiot."

Barnaby leapt up the stone staircase. She was still shouting from down below.

"Go and be a pea picker and live in a shack. See if I care."

Barnaby flew into his room, locking the door behind him. He was unsure of what to do next. He would have to tell Mum that Granny had pickled Dad, but if she didn't believe him, then he would have to run away. He couldn't stay here knowing what he did. He got out a bag and started to throw his clothes in. At the bottom of the drawer was the little brown diary. He still didn't know why his dad had it. There had to be a reason. And he wanted to find out what happened to Mary Morley. He sat on the edge of the bed and carried on reading.

January 12th

I cannot believe that I am writing this diary entry with such a light heart. At the beginning of the day, I thought I would never be happy again. I had spent another night in the forest with just my blanket, too ashamed to return home as my chin now resembles a small gerbil. I was very hungry and ate some of the beetroot while trying to think of a way to get a bogle to kiss me, when I suddenly remembered the folklore chapter in my Big Book of Beetroot. The Romans believed that if a man and a woman ate from the same beetroot they would fall in love. If I could get the brother, Baldric Ballybog, to eat some of my beetroot, I would have no trouble getting him to kiss me. I wasn't sure if it would work on bogles, but it was my only chance.

I jumped into the bog again and was sucked deep down. I shot out, landing on the mossy ground. Thankfully nobody saw me and I crept along to the big house of mud I had been in yesterday. I watched and listened but it looked as if no one was home, so I went inside and hid under the table, which was covered with a large purple cloth, embroidered with gold thread. There I waited, absolutely terrified, clinging to my piece of beetroot. Burpina came in, cooing over her baby. She put her into a tiny backpack, strapped it to her back and left the house. Finally, after what seemed like hours, Baldric Ballybog came in. His hairy feet were centimetres from me as he stood at the table. I was praying for him to make some food. He left the room for a moment and I crept out. My prayers had been answered - there on the table was a huge sandwich. I slipped a shred of my beetroot in and disappeared back under.

He came back in and sat down on a chair, but his foot knocked my knee. He looked under the table, gave a muffled yell and pulled me out by my hair. He was furious, but I could see that his mouth was stuffed full of sandwich. As the food started to go down, so his face became less angry until he was standing there, my hair still in his hands, with a soppy smile on his face. My plan had worked; he was falling in love with me. But what I hadn't realized was that as I watched him swallowing, his face slowly transformed from looking very strange and ugly to very loveable, and I too had a silly, soppy grin on my face. The beetroot had worked both ways. I was in love with a bogle!

Blimey, thought Barnaby. *Beetroot is powerful stuff.*

There was a knock at his door and he leapt off the bed.

"Who is it?" he shouted.

What if it was Granny? He should have made a run for it while he could, instead of reading the diary.

"It's Mum, let me in," she said, rattling the onion knob.

Barnaby unlocked the door.

"Why have you locked the door?" she asked.

"And why aren't you in the cellar with Granny?"

"Mum, we have to get out of here now," he said, ushering her in and locking the door again.

"What's going on, Barnaby? You're scaring me."

"It's Granny; you are not going to believe what she's up to down in that cellar."

"Go on," sighed Mum. She sat down on the bed, a yellowed piece of paper resting in her lap.

"She's pickling all sorts of gruesome things and . . . what's that?"

Mum handed the paper to Barnaby.

"It's her birth certificate. Have a quick look and then I'll pop it back before she notices it's gone. I can't believe I didn't even know my own grandparents' names."

He scanned down the old certificate, looking for the names of Granny's parents.

"Are you OK?" said Mum. "You've gone very pale."

Barnaby stared at the words in horror, unable to believe his eyes. But there it was, in beautiful curly black writing.

NAME:
Beatrix Halitosia Ballybog
PARENTS:
Baldric and Mary Ballybog
PLACE OF BIRTH:
Bogle Bog

Mary Morley had married Baldric Ballybog and changed her name. They were his grandmother's parents. Granny Hogsflesh was half bogle!

CHAPTER 19
The Shocking Truth

"Barnaby, what is it?" asked Mum, taking the birth certificate from his shaking hands.

"Do you know something about Baldric and Mary Ballybog?"

"Mary Ballybog was Mary Morley," he replied, "the owner of **The Big Book of Beetroot**."

"And she was also Granny's mother," said Mum. "So?"

Barnaby pulled the diary from under his pillow and gave it to her.

"Dad dropped this diary just before he disappeared. It also belongs to Mary Morley.

I'm sorry I didn't give it to you sooner," he said, looking at her reproachful face, "but I was worried you would take it away, and I needed to find out the truth."

"The truth about what?" she asked, snatching it off him.

"About our family – the terrible truth about our family. It looks like Mary Morley married a. . ." He couldn't bring himself to say it.

"Barnaby, tell me what you're talking about."

"Mum, you have to read the diary, here, now," he said. "It's Granny, she's a. . ."

"Someone's coming," said Mum. "Listen, footsteps."

"There's no one there. This always happens."

"Of course there's someone there. I can hear them coming," she said, walking to the door.

"You must believe me Mum, it's a . . . bogle."

Mum rolled her eyes to heaven and unlocked

the door. There, standing in the doorway, was Granny Hogsflesh.

Barnaby stared at her big belly and hairy chins. She let out a great belch and suddenly it all made sense. Why had he not guessed before? Everything started clicking into place. Granny had cursed his dad. Then she had pickled the evidence.

"Barnaby, I've come to forgive you for being such an idiot earlier," she said. "I've been thinking it over and—" She stopped dead as she noticed the birth certificate and diary still in Mum's hands. She snatched the diary from her and sat down slowly on the bed.

"Where did you get this?" she whispered.

"It doesn't matter," said Barnaby. "What matters is I have found out your secret, just like Dad did. He confronted you, didn't he – the

night he came home late? And you cursed him
– admit it."

Barnaby was on his feet, shaking with anger.

"You cursed him with the bogle's beard and
then you pickled him."

"I don't know what you're talking about,"
said Granny.

"I don't either," said Mum. "Will somebody
please tell me what is going on?"

"Tell her!" shouted Barnaby. "Tell her what you are."

"Well, maybe I am!" Granny shouted back.

"Maybe you are what?" cried Mum.

"A BOGLE!" Barnaby and Granny shouted together.

Mum looked at them both, her jaw slowly dropping open; then she sank just as slowly on to the floor. Barnaby and Granny hauled her up on to a nearby chair.

"So they do exist," she whispered.

"Of course they exist," said Granny. "They're in our blood, and that stupid man threatened to tell everyone. That information would have ruined me."

Mum stood up at the mention of her husband and Granny took a step backwards.

"What have you done to him?" she asked.

"Don't you understand?" Granny went on,

her voice faltering now. "I had to do something. I didn't want to, but I had no choice. If people found out that bogles existed and that I was only half human, my industry would collapse. I would lose all my power and respect. I might not be able to run for mayor."

Barnaby and Mum glared at her.

"I did it for you two," she said, in an unfamiliar, small voice. She looked at them both, the blood drained from her face.

"What did you do?" hissed Mum. "If you ever want to see Barnaby and me again, you had better start talking."

CHAPTER 20
Confessions

Granny Hogsflesh sat down wearily on the chair. Barnaby had never seen her like this and it felt strange. She seemed smaller.

"He came to me one night," she began. "He showed me my mother's diary and said that he had found out I was only half human and would make it public knowledge if I carried on badgering him to come and work for me. He said he wanted to be independent and to look after his family on his own."

"Mother, that is all we've ever wanted," said Mum. "It doesn't mean we don't want you to be a part of our lives; we just don't want you to control us."

"You don't understand," said Granny. "I have struggled my whole life to fit in. As a child I was never accepted by the bogles because of my human mother, and so I tried to fit in to her world – the human world. It was hard. People are suspicious of women with hairy chins, but I did it. I worked hard, I married a human, I made a lot of money and earned the respect and the power that I have always deserved. Then that man came along and threatened to take it all away."

"He didn't want to take anything away," said Mum. "He just didn't want to work for you."

"He didn't want you to work for me either," said Granny, "or Barnaby. What about my pickles? I'm getting old and I need someone to take over from me."

"That's not true," said Mum. "*I* didn't want

to work for you. I don't like pickling, and as for Barnaby, well, it's totally up to him."

"And that shack," Granny continued. "I couldn't bear seeing you living in that shack."

"But we were happy," said Mum. "Don't you understand? This big house means nothing. We were happy in our 'shack'."

Granny looked down.

"So you put the curse of the bogle's beard on him," said Barnaby.

She continued to look at the floor.

"And then you pickled him."

Granny looked up sharply. "For once and for all, I have not pickled your father," she said. "Those were baboon bones, a gift from a Gibraltarian client. You worked yourself up into a state about nothing."

She looked like she was telling the truth and Barnaby felt slightly foolish.

"Well, where is he, then?" he asked.

"I don't know for certain. . ." said Granny.

"What does the curse of the bogle's beard do to you?" asked Mum.

"It makes you start to look and behave like a bogle," said Barnaby. "Bad manners, bad beard and bad wind."

"The curse meant nothing," said Granny. "It was just meant to scare him, to show him how powerful I am, so he wouldn't threaten me again. The curse can be broken by a kiss from a bogle, or a half bogle, or even a quarter bogle. The minute he came home and kissed you, Hatty, he would have been OK."

"Oh my goodness, I'm a bogle," said Mum, sitting down suddenly.

"I didn't know he was going to leave home," said Granny, "and when he did, I thought it was because he couldn't handle a bogle family.

I thought you had been abandoned, and that suited me."

"Did Grandpa Hogsflesh know that you were a bogle?" asked Barnaby.

Granny looked uncomfortable.

"The subject never came up," she said.

"And if it had," he continued, "would he have left you?"

"Of course not," she said. "Your grandfather was a fine man and he would never have abandoned his . . . family."

"Exactly," said Barnaby. "Nor would my dad."

"I see what you're saying," said Granny.

"But why didn't he tell us?" said Mum. "Why did he go off on his own without a word?"

Granny looked down at the floor again.

"Mother?" said Mum sharply.

"I told him that I knew lots of bogle curses,"

said Granny, "and that if he ever told you what had happened, then the next one would be much worse."

"Is that true?" asked Barnaby.

"No," said Granny. "I didn't even know I could do that one. Worked quite well, though. . ."

Mum and Barnaby glared at her.

"I mean . . . *unfortunately* it worked quite. . . Anyway, I think we should be thinking about where he is now. If he hasn't abandoned you, then where has he gone?"

"He's read the diary," said Barnaby. "So he knows that the only way to break the curse is by a bogle kiss. He must have gone looking for them, just like Mary Morley."

"Well then, there is only one place he can be," said Granny, quietly. "Bogle Bog. We must go to the Forest of Fen. I will explain everything on the way."

CHAPTER 21
Back to the Bog

Barnaby wrapped his jacket tightly around him as a cold wind blew. They all left town and headed towards the forest in the distance. Granny Hogsflesh was walking a few paces behind them. She now looked very different from the loud, bossy old woman barking orders.

He almost felt sorry for her until he remembered what she had done. They passed their old wooden house. It looked strange and lonely. It seemed like a lifetime had gone by since he had been there, so much had happened. He felt Mum give his hand a reassuring squeeze as they walked by.

"Won't be long now," she whispered. "We're not coming back without Dad."

He could feel the butterflies rising in his stomach and was not sure if it was excitement or nerves. He turned as Granny caught them up. She was looking back at their old house.

"I know that I kept calling your old home a shed and a shack," she said. "But it brings back bad memories for me. You see, I used to live there."

"You never told me that," said Mum in surprise. "You've lied to me all these years? Where exactly did you grow up?"

"I grew up in Bogle Bog," she sighed. "I hated it, I never fitted in properly, and I wanted to make something of myself. My parents died of marsh fever when I was eighteen and I went to tell my human grandparents, who lived in the shack – or beetroot farm, as they liked to call it. As horrible as it was, it was much better than living in the bog, so I decided to stay and work on the farm. It was hard work and the problem was. . ."

"Nobody likes beetroot?" interrupted Barnaby.

"Exactly," she said. "And I didn't intend to dig up beetroot for the rest of my life. So I persuaded my grandparents to ditch the beetroot and invest in a chicken. Soon one chicken became two, then three, until I had built up a successful poultry farm. We were much better off, but it wasn't enough. I wanted more. I wanted to be rich."

"So what did you do?" asked Barnaby.

"Harry Hogsflesh lived on the onion farm next door."

"Don't you mean *Ho-flay*?" said Mum.

"He pronounced it Hogsflesh at that time. But I soon changed that, the minute I married him. We needed a grand name to go with my grand plans. His farm was much bigger than ours and I could see its potential for making money. The problem was how to get it. He wasn't interested in me. My farm was small, and he never looked twice at me – must have been the hairy chin. Anyway, my mother, Mary Morley, had told me all about the power of beetroot. So I did what she had done. I forced myself to eat a piece of beetroot and slipped the rest into Harry Hogsflesh's sandwich one day."

"How could that help?" asked Mum.

"The Romans believed that beetroot had magical qualities," Barnaby explained, "and if a man and woman ate the same beetroot, they would fall in love."

"You tricked him," said Mum, shocked. "I thought you actually loved each other."

"We did," said Granny, defensively. "Love comes to people in many different ways. Does it matter how it happened? I began to pickle my eggs and his onions and that was the start of everything. The more I pickled, the more money I made. The more money I made, the more powerful I became, and the more powerful I became, the more accepted I was in the human world."

They were nearing the forest now and Barnaby was feeling very nervous.

"Do you still know any bogles that live here, Granny?" he asked.

"Yes, I do," she said, stiffly. "My cousin, Belchetta Ballybog. We grew up together; she was just a couple of years older than me."

"Belchetta?" he asked. "The baby that your mother found, that started the whole curse in the first place?"

"That's right. How did you know that?"

"I read it in the diary," he said.

"Ah, yes, my mother's diary," she said, bitterly. "Belchetta has tormented me for years. She despised me for leaving Bogle Bog and when I married a human she was mad with jealousy. Belchetta was left behind in the swamp. That bogle visits my house every day, making a mess in my rooms and strange noises round corners. You heard her one day, Barnaby, do you remember?"

"I heard her lots of days," said Barnaby. "And she must have made the mess in my room."

"Of course," said Granny. "I'd forgotten about that."

They reached the edge of the Forest of Fen.

Granny led them through the trees to a clearing. In the middle was an enormous sludgy-green bog. It smelled of rotten meat mixed with manure. Barnaby could hardly breathe.

"Here we are," said Granny. "I haven't been here in many years. All you have to do is jump in. You will be sucked down into Bogle Bog."

"All we have to do is jump in?" repeated Mum, faintly. "There is no way I am jumping in that. You do it."

"I'm afraid I can't," said Granny. "I was banished for ever, for turning my back on the bogle community. It's impossible for me to

return. If I jumped in, I would just sink and drown."

"Well, maybe that's what you deserve," said Mum, angrily. "If you hadn't cursed my husband, then we wouldn't be standing here now, about to jump into a huge puddle of poo, trying to find him."

Granny turned and walked a little way away. She tried to say something, but a big gust of wind shook the trees overhead, carrying her voice away and sending down a small shower of leaves.

"What did she say?" asked Mum.

"I think she said she was sorry," said Barnaby.

"Impossible," said Mum. "She's never said sorry in her life."

"Must have been the wind," he said.

"OK, Barnaby, hold my hand. We'll jump in together." Barnaby felt like his heart was trying to hammer its way through his ribs and escape. He could hardly hear what his mum was saying. He held her hand and looked down at the greeny-brown mush and then turned to his granny. Her body was bowed and her head hung down.

"I hope for your sake we find him," shouted Mum. "Ready, Barnaby? One, two, three . . .

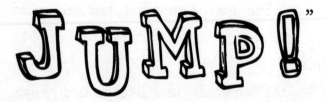

"

CHAPTER 22
Bogle Bog

They jumped in together, expecting to sink immediately, but it was a slow process. The bog only came up to their knees, and then little by little they began to go under. Barnaby's grip on his mum's hand tightened as the bog rose to his waist. She gave him what was supposed to be an encouraging smile but looked more like a grimace.

"It's OK," she said, in a strange high voice. "Don't worry, darling."

Barnaby could feel the cold marsh seeping through his clothes to his bare skin and he started to shiver. The smell was unbearable. Great globs of green pulp oozed through the brown slush, gradually reaching his neck. His mum was being sucked away from him and they lost hold of each other's hands. She was up to her chest. Barnaby felt it rising over his chin and started to panic. He couldn't move his limbs. He was going to die.

"MUM," he screamed. "Help me, Mu. . ." He shut his mouth abruptly as some cold, squelchy liquid seeped in. He just had time to see his mother's horrified face as he was pulled completely under.

The icy sludge enveloped his face. He had no breath left in his body and just as he thought his lungs would explode, the mud opened out around his head, forming a bubble. He gratefully breathed in the stinking air. But he was still being sucked in, lower and lower, gathering speed the deeper he went. He travelled faster, vertical drops followed by steep spirals, down and down. His hair stood on end and his face was pulled back with the force. He opened his mouth to scream but suddenly shot out of the bog, flew through the air and landed in a heap on a mossy mound.

He lay on his back for a moment, unable to move. All around was a foul boggy stench. Slowly his surroundings came into focus. He was in a gigantic cave of mud, as tall as a cathedral, with tree roots protruding from the ceiling. Strange holes dotted a rock face high above. He got up and looked around. Bogle Bog. It was just as Mary Morley had described in her diary. Nothing seemed to have changed in all those years. Burning lamps dimly lit up the round houses, which looked like giant Maltesers, snaking out in all directions along narrow winding paths. The mud-ball houses around him were laid out to form three sides of a large square, the rock face with the holes in making the fourth.

Barnaby jumped at the sound of a scream above him. He looked up to see his mum fly out of one of the holes in the rock above and land on another bed of moss with a thud. He ran over to her.

"Mum?" he asked anxiously. "Are you all right?"

"All right?" she gasped. "I'll never be all right again."

"It's OK," said Barnaby. "We've made it, we're here."

Mum looked around slowly in disbelief and wrinkled her nose.

"First I find out that bogles are real," she panted. "Then I discover that I am related to them; then I'm sucked down into a filthy, stinking bog and rocketed through the ground at over a hundred miles an hour into a dark underground world that smells like a rotten camel. I don't think I can take much more."

"Of course you can," said Barnaby, trying to snap her out of the daze she was in. "We haven't even found Dad yet."

"You're right," she said, dusting herself down.

"I need to be a bit braver – like you."

Barnaby couldn't hide his smile.

"Look," said Mum. "We're not even a bit muddy. How strange."

"I know," he said. "I don't understand. . . Shh . . . there's someone coming."

CHAPTER 23
Meeting Bogles

They crouched down behind a large rock as a bogle came into the square with a baby on her back. Barnaby and Mum stared. It was the first bogle they had ever seen. She looked quite pretty from behind, with long dark hair tied on top like a pineapple and her baby bobbing up and down behind her. She paused and looked around as if she could feel she was being watched. Her mouth was curled in a horrible scowl and several long black hairs dangled from her chin. A dirty grey rag serving as a dress hung over her pot belly and two skinny little legs dropped down to the largest, hairiest feet Barnaby had ever seen. The baby behind her did indeed look like a beetroot, just as Mary Morley had thought. After a moment she turned and started on her way again.

"OK, what now?" whispered Mum.

"We have to find Belchetta's house," said Barnaby. "She's the only one who might help us find Dad. We're just going to have to talk to them."

"Right, then," said Mum. "Feeling brave?"

Barnaby paused for a moment, then looked up at her determinedly.

"Actually, I am," he said.

They came out from behind the rock and called after the bogle mother.

"Excuse me," he said, loudly. The bogle turned and burped noisily, her mouth hanging open. "We were wondering if. . ."

"Humans," spat the little creature.

"Yes, we are," he said, trying not to sound scared. "We were wondering if you could. . ."

"Humans!" she cried again and ran off, with her beetroot baby bouncing up and down behind her.

Several bogles came out of nearby houses to see what was going on, and more approached from adjoining streets. They glared at the newcomers as the square began to fill.

Barnaby remembered that Mary Morley had been surrounded in the square and quickly pulled his mum up a narrow gravel path.

"Let's get out of here," he said.

There was no grass or plants, just earth and roots. The occasional sludgy drip would fall from the high ceiling above and splat on the ground around them. The dim lamps hardly gave out any light and it was difficult to see too far ahead. Barnaby felt engulfed in muddy brown. It was also very hot. He took his jacket off and tied it round his waist.

"I know from reading the diary that Belchetta used to live in one of the biggest houses here," he said, trying not to let the heat and the brown get to him. "It was about six balls big. She might still be there – or at least whoever lives there might know where to find her."

Several more bogles loomed up out of the

darkness and stopped to stare at them, their black eyes glinting with suspicion. Barnaby was so nervous he couldn't look at them, but Mum put on her best fake smile.

"Good afternoon," she said, pleasantly. "Lovely village you have here."

The bogles glared back, their hairy little faces pinched with hostility.

"You shouldn't be here," said the largest one.

"Well, if you could possibly help us, then we won't stay long. We're looking for—"

"Help?" he interrupted. "Help a human?" His red hair framed the whole of his face and he looked like an angry orang-utan. "We don't help humans. Now get out of here."

"OK," smiled Mum. "We'll be off, then."

She pulled Barnaby round a corner. They squeezed between two houses away from the unfriendly group of bogles.

"The locals aren't overly helpful," she said, wiping the sweat from her face.

They came out on to a bigger street with a long mud house taking up most of it. There was a large main ball with five round pods joined to it. A circular front door lay open.

"Six balls big," said Mum.

"What do we do?" said Barnaby. "We can't knock and there's no bell."

Mum put her head close to the door and called, "Coo-ee, is there anyone home?"

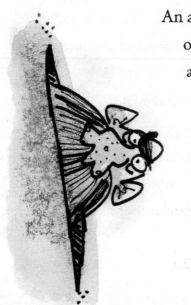

An angry head popped out of a round hole, serving as a window. The black eyes opened wide at the sight of Barnaby andhis mum, then narrowed with distrust.

"Not more of you," he shouted. "Get lost." And the head disappeared inside.

"More of you?" repeated Barnaby. "Surely humans don't visit here very often."

"That is strange," said Mum. "Anyway, it doesn't look like he was going to help us. Let's see if we can find another big house."

They tramped all around the mud-ball houses, trying to keep to the shadows whenever a bogle passed by. Barnaby was covered in smelly splats of bog that had fallen on him from above. He was beginning to feel very fed up.

"We can't just wander around aimlessly," he said. "This is hopeless."

"What shall we do?" said Mum. She too was covered in blotches of bog. "No one will help us, we don't know where we're going, it's dark, it's hot, it's smelly, it's. . ."

She broke off as a bogle clambered out through

the front hole of a large house set back from the others. She was clearly old, and so bent that the hairs on her chin tickled the top of her round belly.

Barnaby and Mum backed into the shadows, but it was too late; she had seen them.

"Who's there?" she called in a high-pitched voice.

They stepped out into the light of a lamp. The ancient bogle looked up and the three of them stood staring at one another in shock. There was no getting away from the family resemblance. The old bogle was the image of Granny Hogsflesh. And the recognition in her eyes told them that they had at last found Belchetta Ballybog.

CHAPTER 24
Belchetta Ballybog

Barnaby wouldn't have believed that anyone could be uglier than Granny Hogsflesh. That was until he met her cousin. She wasn't as tall or as wide as Granny, but she had the same long bent nose and thick lips. Large patches of bald scalp showed through the wisps and tufts of her grey hair. Her wrinkled old skin had a purple hue and she reminded Barnaby of the beetroot baby they had seen earlier. Her dirty grey dress was stretched tight over a huge belly, and her thin knobbly legs were supported by two big bony feet.

"Come to visit the poor relatives, have we?" she croaked. "Had enough of the big purple mansion, have we?" The hatred in her eyes took Barnaby by surprise.

"Belchetta?" asked Barnaby, nervously. "You obviously know who we are."

The wrinkled old bogle looked them both up and down.

"We've come to ask for your help," said Mum.

"Your face," Belchetta said, completely ignoring Barnaby's mum and poking a long crooked finger at him. "Your face, when you saw that I'd wrecked your room."

She laughed uproariously, like she had just told the funniest joke in the world, and then stopped immediately. "You didn't know it was a bogle, did you?" she said. "You didn't even know we existed."

She spat the last words out, hatred filling her horrible little face.

"I'm sorry," said Barnaby. "It's just . . . I was never told about them . . . told about you."

"Why didn't you tell the boy where he comes from?" she squawked, turning to his mum.

"Because I didn't know either," said Mum,

pulling Barnaby closer to her.

"Well, well," Belchetta said to herself. "My dear cousin, Beatrix Hogsflesh, didn't even tell her own daughter. She was so ashamed of us; she pretended we didn't even exist."

Barnaby could see a bright purple vein on Belchetta's neck bulging out and throbbing angrily.

"I won't let her forget where she comes from," she said. "I visit her regularly. She never sees, but she knows it's me, doing what bogles do best – tormenting humans."

Barnaby and Mum were taken aback by the scale of Belchetta's emotions. They were not expecting this. She was in full rant, and there was no stopping her.

"We used to be close," she said. "We grew up together and would sneak up into the human world. That's when she started to get her high and mighty ideas."

Belchetta sat down on a large rock. "Started to look down on us, she did. Wanted to marry a human and live above ground. I told her that a human would never look twice at a bogle."

She started to imitate Granny's voice. "But I'm not a bogle, Belchetta, you are. I'm half human and I don't belong underground."

Belchetta burped angrily. Barnaby and Mum remained silent, keen to hear the whole story. She glared at them before continuing.

"I wanted to live above ground too, to wake up in the sunlight, not under these miserable burning lamps. When her parents died, it was the perfect excuse for her to leave here. She knew I wanted to come with her but she said she had to go alone and would come back for me. But she never did. My mother, Burpina, was right about her. She was a scheming liar. Once she met that

Hogsflesh human, that was it. I often wondered how she managed to marry him. She never told me about her little beetroot trick. But then I found out how she did it. I found her mother's diary."

CHAPTER 25
Dead End

"It was you who gave my dad the diary," gasped Barnaby.

"Of course it was me, you little twerp," snapped Belchetta. "He had a right to know about the family he had married into. He needed to find out the truth about his dear mother-in-law. I let him know that we were related and it didn't take him long to put two and two together after he read the diary."

"Belchetta, I'm sorry for the way my mother treated you," said Mum. "I'm sorry that you got left behind in the bog, but I need to find my husband."

"Gone missing, has he?" she asked.

"Yes," said Barnaby urgently. "My granny put the curse of the bogle's beard on him and we thought he might have come here to the village."

"Needed a kiss from a bogle to break the curse, did he?" she chuckled. "I did see him. . ."

"When?"

"The day I visited the pea farm and gave him the diary. That was the last time I saw him. He was never here in the village."

Barnaby's eyes burned as he tried to hold back the tears.

"Belchetta, please," said Mum. "Have you any idea where else he could have gone? Is there another bogle community somewhere?"

The old bogle started to walk back into her house.

"There are hundreds of bogles in this country," she said. "He could be anywhere. I expect he just ran away after finding out the truth about his family. I doubt you will ever see him again."

And she disappeared into her giant Malteser house.

Mum put her arm around Barnaby. They turned and started to walk back along the gravel path.

"What if she's right?" sniffed Barnaby. "What if he never comes back?"

"Your dad would never leave us," she said, holding him closer. "He needs our help and if we have to search every bog in the country, we will."

They went on silently back to the village square. It was quiet again and they rushed across and crouched behind the same large rock they had hidden behind before.

"How do we get out of this place?" asked Mum, looking up at the holes in the rock high above.

"According to the diary," said Barnaby, "there's a long ladder which leads up into a hollow tree – if it's still here."

As they looked around, a small bogle child shot out of one of the holes, flew over their heads and landed on the soft bed of moss.

"Woohoo!" he shouted, not noticing the visitors crouching behind him.

"Hello," said Barnaby, peering round the rock. "Could you tell me how to get out of here?"

The little bogle spun round and eyed them up and down.

"I'm not supposed to help humans," he said.

"Do you get a lot of humans here, then?" asked Barnaby, in surprise.

"No," he said. "Just one other – a big man with red hair, a green hat and a beard just like ours."

"Where did you see him?" asked Barnaby,

shooting his mum a look.

"There," said the child, pointing back down the gravel path. "He was with Belchetta Ballybog."

CHAPTER 26

The Prisoner

By the time they returned to Belchetta's house, she had gone. They climbed through the doorway shouting Dad's name. The large spherical room was dominated by a round table covered with a thick purple cloth embroidered with gold. Three bronze shields hung from the walls. They looked like they were intricately embossed, but Barnaby didn't have time to look. He dashed through one of three holes that led off from the main room. His mum disappeared through another, still shouting his dad's name. He found himself in a perfectly round kitchen, with small wooden

cupboards curving all the way around. It was empty. He heard his mum calling him and headed back out, following her voice through one of the other holes, which led to an inner corridor. Two round doors were set into the wall, one of which was lying open. Barnaby's mum was inspecting a large bolt attached to it.

"Dad was here," she shouted.

Inside was a small bed with a pea-green hat lying on top.

"Look, his hat. He's been locked up in this room," said Barnaby.

They ran back through the house.

"He can't be far away," said Mum. "She must have made a run for it and taken him with her."

They stood outside for a moment, looking around.

"Which way?" cried Barnaby, frantically.

A pair of scruffy bogles came along the path and stopped to stare at them.

"Have you seen Belchetta Ballybog?" asked Mum, desperately.

"No," said the first one. "And even if I had, I wouldn't tell a human."

"I am not a human!" she yelled, picking one of them up and holding him level with her face. "I am a quarter bogle!"

She was shrieking, even though his face was only centimetres from hers.

"Belchetta is my second cousin and you better tell me where I can find her, bogle boy, or I shall turn you upside down and shake you till your nasty yellow teeth drop out."

The bogle looked terrified and his friend ran away. Barnaby had never seen his mum like this – he was impressed.

"There's only one other place she ever goes to," he whimpered. "She has a human cousin. She loves to go above ground and torment her."

"Quick," said Barnaby, "back to Granny's house."

Mum dropped the bogle and he started to run away but she caught hold of the back of his collar.

"One last thing," she growled. "How do we get out of here?"

He pointed to where they could just make out a long ladder stretching to the roof of the cavern.

They raced through the narrow paths to the bottom of the ladder, ignoring the shouts and glares from passing bogles. Barnaby looked up, and his knees felt suddenly weak. It must have been as high as three or four houses.

"M-Mum," he stuttered. "You know I don't like heights."

"This is not the time, Barnaby," she barked. "Your dad is at the top of that ladder. Now get a move on."

He wasn't sure if he liked or disliked his mum's new mood – impressive, but scary. She was right, though; now was not the time to be afraid. He had to find his courage, so he began to climb.

CHAPTER 27
The Search

Eventually they reached the hollow tree and pulled themselves up and out. Barnaby sucked in great lungfuls of fresh air.

The rotting smell from below seemed to cling to his nostrils.

They sat there for a moment sweating, despite the cold night, the moonlight piercing the branches above. Mum put her arm around him.

"Well done, Barnaby," she said. "I knew you could do it."

He smiled to himself – yes, he could do it. After catching their breath, they set off again through the Forest of Fen, running past their old house, into the town and finally to Granny Hogsflesh's mansion.

"Dad?" shouted Barnaby, running from room to room. "Granny?"

He could hear his mum upstairs. "Fergus? Belchetta? Mother?"

It took a long time to search the great house and they finally met each other on the stairs, exhausted.

"Anything?" asked Mum, breathing heavily.

"No," panted Barnaby. "No Dad, no Belchetta and no Granny. Where is she?"

He lay back on the stairs, drained.

"They've got to be here," said Mum, "but where?"

Barnaby sat up suddenly. There was one place they hadn't checked.

"The cellar," he said. "Come on, quick."

He led her down the stone staircase to the large door.

"You know, I've never been in here," said Mum, nervously. "Granny tried to persuade me to come in with her when I was younger, but I never wanted to. Silly, I suppose."

"Not silly at all," said Barnaby, pulling the key out and sticking it into the lamp above. "You just wait till you see what she's got in here."

The control panel dropped down and he typed in 666. The large door sank into the floor to reveal the second one. Barnaby pressed his eyes to the scanners and it lifted up. His mum slipped in behind him before both doors slid back into place. They were in the long, dark room. Slowly they crept towards the different pickling caves and the great vats of vinegar.

"Toenails?" read Mum, in disgust.

"It gets worse," said Barnaby, quietly. He thought he had seen something move at the end of the room in the experimental section.

"Mucus and earwax?" she said, faintly. "I don't believe it."

Barnaby stopped by the vats of bubbling animal gases, straining to see if he had actually seen something.

"Can we please move on?" said Mum, holding her nose. "I think I'm going to be sick."

"Shh," he whispered. "I think I saw someone."

They crept forward into the next section.

"I cannot believe I am hiding behind a huge jar of pickled verrucas," she sighed.

"Shh," he breathed, grabbing her arm.

There in the experimental room opposite the beetroot, dirty and dishevelled and tied to a chair, was his father.

"Dad!" cried Barnaby, running towards him.

Dad looked up, his eyes wide with horror.

"No, Barnaby!" he shouted. "Stay back!"

CHAPTER 28
Belchetta's Plan

It was too late. Barnaby felt an arm around his neck and was dragged to the ground from behind. Belchetta Ballybog looked bigger than the last time they had seen her and she had the power of a grown man. He guessed she had taken some of the pickled earwax, to give her strength.

"Stay back," she screamed, as Mum came running forward, "or I'll toenail him."

In her grubby little hand was a large yellow toenail, curled and wrinkled with age. She pressed it to Barnaby's throat and he could smell its foul, cheesy odour.

"One prick from this little thing will shrivel him up like a raisin," she said, keeping her eyes on Barnaby's mum.

Mum looked unsure, but stopped still.

"It's true," croaked Barnaby, trying to get a breath as Belchetta still held him tightly round the neck. "It's poisonous; all these pickles are used in black magic."

"Now," Belchetta barked, "sit in that chair next to your husband."

Mum sat down slowly. "What do you want with us?" she cried.

"All in good time," said Belchetta, tying Barnaby to a chair opposite with one hand and keeping the toenail close to his throat with the other. The rope cut into his wrists. He could hear his mum and dad whispering.

"I'm sorry, Fergus."

"None of this is your fault," said Dad. "I got trapped in the bogle world. That old creature said she had plans for me." He nodded towards Belchetta. "Eventually, she said she would take me back above ground. She told me you and Barnaby were waiting for me here. She had keys to your mother's house. They're cousins."

"I know," said Mum.

"I bet that old goat is behind all this," said Dad. "She's wanted me out of the way for years."

"I know what Mother did to you," began

Mum. "I've heard all about the curse of the bogle's beard, but I don't think she would—"

But Dad wouldn't let her finish. "How else could Belchetta get inside here?" he said. "She knew the code to get in; she scanned her eyes and pulled me in behind her."

Belchetta looked up at the sound of her name. "How sweet," she said, tying the last knot round Barnaby's wrist, "together again after all this time."

She put the toenail down and picked up more rope to tie Mum to her chair. "Make the most of it," she cackled, "because he will soon be your ex-husband."

Quick as a flash, Mum leapt from her chair, pinning Belchetta to the ground. Belchetta screeched in fury and rolled over so she was now on top. Barnaby struggled to get free as his mum and Belchetta wrestled on the floor. She had only

tied the knot around his wrist with one hand and it was starting to feel slightly loose. He pulled and wriggled desperately. But earwax mixed with mucus had given Belchetta great power and soon the shrivelled old bogle had secured Barnaby's mum to the chair. Mum screamed in frustration as Belchetta picked up the yellow toenail.

"Quiet," she shouted, waving it in the air. "Or I'll turn you into a prune."

She held the toenail close to his mum's pale cheek. Barnaby held his breath and stopped wriggling. Belchetta laughed horribly before dropping the toenail back into a jar.

"Not today," she said. "After all, you are family. And anyway, I want you to watch the show."

"What show?" demanded Dad.

"*Our* show, my handsome husband," said Belchetta, putting her craggy face close to his. Dad recoiled in disgust.

"What are you talking about?" said Mum. "He's my husband."

"Not for much longer," said Belchetta, disappearing into the beetroot section. "He's going to leave you and Barnaby and marry me."

Barnaby and his parents watched in confusion as she emerged, triumphantly holding a jar of pickled beetroot.

"My cousin left me behind in the bog," she said, "while she married a human and lived above ground in a huge mansion. Well, now it's my turn."

"What do you mean?" asked Dad.

"You and I shall eat from the same beetroot, and fall in love," she said. "You will leave your present wife and child and marry me."

Barnaby and his parents stared at one another in horror.

"But you hate humans," cried Barnaby.

"But I love tormenting them," she cackled. "And if it means I can live above ground in the sun, in a big fancy house, then I am willing to do anything."

"But I haven't got a big fancy house," said Dad.

"No, but my cousin has," she said. "But first things first, let's eat some beetroot."

A cold, sick feeling washed over Barnaby. He had lost his dad once. He couldn't let it happen again.

CHAPTER 29
The Old Beetroot Trick

"You can't do this," yelled Dad, struggling to get free.

"Oh yes I can," said Belchetta, holding the jar up to the light and studying the beetroot inside.

"I won't eat it!" he cried.

"Oh yes you will," she smiled, unscrewing the jar.

"Why are you doing this?" asked Barnaby, still wriggling his hands madly together in a bid to get free. "You must be at least seventy. You're too old for him."

"Bogles live a lot longer than humans, young

man. We'll have years together. And if I were you, I'd be a lot more polite to your future stepmother."

She pulled out several chunks of beetroot from the jar and started stuffing them into her mouth, the purple juice running down her chin.

"Why should Beatrix Hogsflesh have it all?" she said in a muffled voice. "It's not too late for me to marry a human and live above ground too," she spat, spraying beetroot everywhere. "Why shouldn't I use the same beetroot trick that she and her human mother, Mary Morley, used to get what they wanted?"

"But why me?" asked Dad.

"I gave you that diary so you could ruin my cousin, but you failed. Then you walked into our village looking for a bogle to kiss you and break the curse. Once you eat this beetroot, I can kiss you, so you get what you want ... and I get what

I want – the same life as Beatrix Hogsflesh."

She took a step closer to him.

"Now, open wide," she said, trying to stuff some beetroot in his mouth. Dad shook his head from side to side, trying to get away from her.

"Wait!" shouted Barnaby, trying to buy his dad more time. "How did you find out about the cellar? How did you get in here?"

"I know every inch of this house. I have been coming here for years," she said. "I've read all the pickled potion books down here, and some of these recipes were stolen from my mother, Burpina. I know everything there is to know about dark pickles. Your granny thought she could keep me out with her fancy locks and eye scanners, but you can't lock a bogle out; they can get in anywhere."

She turned back towards Dad. "Now, where were we?" she leered. "Oh yes, open wide."

She was dangling a piece of droopy beetroot in front of his mouth.

"Never," he shouted, thrashing from left to right. But she was too strong for him. She held his head still and pinched his nose so he had to open his mouth to breathe. In went the beetroot. As she was putting her large knobbly hand over his mouth to stop him from spitting it out, there was a crash behind them. They all spun around as Granny Hogsflesh came thundering through the doors, her face as purple as the juice running down Belchetta's chin.

"Get away from my family!" she roared.

CHAPTER 30
The Battle of the Bogles

Belchetta's hand fell from Dad's mouth. He spat out the beetroot, which flew through the air and landed on her cheek.

"I'm doing you a favour, dear Beatrix," she said, peeling the beetroot off her face. "You've always wanted rid of him. Now is your chance. All it will take is one small bite of beetroot —" she waved the wet, purple sliver in the air —"and you never have to see him again. The other two will be all yours."

Granny Hogsflesh looked at her daughter, then at Barnaby. He locked eyes with her. He knew she was rude to everyone and had lots of horrible habits, but he also began to realize that she cared a lot for him and Mum.

"He's a fool, Beatrix," Belchetta pressed on. "You said so yourself."

"Well, I was. . ." Granny Hogsflesh seemed to choke on her words. "I was wro. . ." She couldn't quite get them out. "I was . . . WRONG," she shouted. "He is not a fool. He is my daughter's husband and my grandson's dad and you are not having him."

Barnaby felt a warm feeling grow deep in his stomach as he watched his granny storm over to Belchetta and snatch the beetroot from her hand, flinging it across the room.

"I've done some horrible things in my life," she said, her nose centimetres away from her cousin's, "but now it's my chance to make up for it."

Belchetta backed off slowly. "Then you are

the fool," she said, edging her way towards the animal gases. "This is my chance to leave the bog for ever." She reached behind her, still facing them all. "And I intend to take it, even if it means pickling the lot of you."

She grabbed a glass jar and hurled it at Granny. It smashed against the huge vat behind her. A thin green vapour snaked through the air from the broken jar, reaching Barnaby's nose a second later. A terrible stench settled around him. He held his breath and struggled furiously against the rough ropes that cut into his arms. He was nearly free, but ran out of air and had to take a great gulp of the foul green gas. He felt it burning his mouth and throat, all the way down to his lungs. He started coughing furiously, but instead of a cough, out came a snort. He was snorting madly, unable to control himself. He could also hear his parents snorting wildly.

"It's a burp from the Indo-Chinese Warty Pig," shouted Granny Hogsflesh out of the green mist. "We're lucky; it will wear off in about two minutes."

Eyes streaming and nose numb with snorting, Barnaby didn't feel very lucky.

"If it was a burp from the Java Warty Pig, we'd have been in real trouble," she yelled.

The foggy burp started to subside and Barnaby could make out the figures of his mum and dad still tied to their chairs opposite him, their faces the colour of a stagnant pond. The snorting had stopped and Granny was kneeling behind Dad, furiously trying to untie him.

"I know you can never forgive me for what I have done," she said, fumbling with the ropes behind, "but we have to work together to get Belchettaaaaagggghhh."

Barnaby watched as Belchetta leapt on to Granny's shoulders. Her skinny little legs wrapped around Granny's fat neck and her wobbly tummy bounced against the back of Granny's head like a pillow.

"Get her off, get her off!" Granny shouted, staggering around blindly as Belchetta's hands covered her eyes.

"I've got you now," cried Belchetta, squeezing her legs tight around Granny's neck. Granny stumbled out of sight into the pickled verruca room. Barnaby and his mum and dad watched helplessly as they re-emerged, Granny holding a jar. Her face had turned puce as Belchetta continued squeezing, but with great effort she lifted the jar in front of her face and smashed it up against Belchetta's forehead.

CHAPTER 31
Betrayal

Slowly Belchetta released her grip and slid down Granny's back.

"What have you done to me?" she whispered in a daze, falling to the floor. A trickle of blood ran down her face from a small cut on her head. It was mixed with the slime that was inside the smashed jar.

"Vole verrucas," said Granny, still gasping for breath. "Small but highly effective. That should keep you quiet until we've worked out what to do with you."

"What are we going to do with her?" asked Barnaby.

"I'm not sure yet," said Granny, "but the pickled vole verrucas will have entered her bloodstream through the cut on her head, and will remove all her strength and energy, giving us time to get untied and think of a plan."

"Beatrix," whispered Belchetta weakly from the floor. "I'm sorry. I just wanted to be like you."

"Humph," muttered Granny, making her way towards Barnaby.

"Beatrix, please," said the small voice. "We all make mistakes; we all need second chances. You know that better than anyone. I need to apologize."

Granny Hogsflesh stopped and slowly turned to her cousin.

"Well . . . I suppose. . ." she began.

"Come closer," breathed Belchetta. "I hardly have the strength to talk."

Granny hesitated before walking back to where she lay.

"Closer," she whispered.

Granny knelt down and bent over the sprawled figure.

"Beatrix," she sighed, slowly putting her arm around Granny's neck. "Never trust a . . . bogle."

She was holding something between her thumb and forefinger. Barnaby strained to see what it was. His eyes widened in fear as he recognized the wrinkled yellow toenail.

"GRANNY, WATCH OUT!" he screamed.

But before Granny realized what was happening, Belchetta had stabbed it into her neck. She sank to the floor beside Belchetta, who scraped the vole verrucas off her head and sat up, laughing loudly.

"You stupid . . . trusting . . . old fool," she said, her voice slightly slurred. "It must be the h-h-human in you."

Belchetta staggered to her feet, still half dazed, and fell against the table.

"Well, well, well," she said, nudging Granny's crumpled body with her foot. "The mighty Beatrix Hogsflesh has gone . . . sooner than I had planned."

She turned and stared at Barnaby and Mum, her black eyes glinting malevolently.

"If you two were also to go . . . that would leave this huge house and the Hogsflesh Pickle Company, all to her nearest relative. . . I believe that would be . . . ME."

She held the toenail up in front of her, still swaying slightly from the effects of the vole verrucas.

"So who's next?" she smiled, looking round at them. "Mummy or baby Barnaby?"

"I won't let you do it!" yelled Dad, fighting

furiously against the ropes that bound him.

"After you've eaten your beetroot," she said, "you'll be so in love with me that you won't care what I do. And if you do give me any problems, then I'll toenail you too."

Barnaby looked at the body of his grandmother slumped on the floor, a choking feeling rising in his chest.

"Granny?" he whispered.

"She can't help you now, little boy," said Belchetta, trying unsuccessfully to walk towards him. "And you are next. Fortunately for you, my strength hasn't returned yet. I need some more pickled earwax."

She lurched towards the huge vat in the middle of the room, grabbing an empty jar on the way.

"I'll get some of the fresh stuff," she said.

Barnaby watched as she climbed unsteadily to the top of the ladder. His hands were nearly free. His wrists were cut and bleeding from struggling for so long, but he had to get to Granny Hogsflesh.

"Just one little cup of this," said Belchetta from the top of the vat, "and I'll be back to my old self."

The rope around his hands dropped to the floor. Barnaby signalled to his mum and dad that he was free. He kept his eyes on Belchetta, who was dipping the jar into the enormous tank of pickled earwax. He quietly slid to the floor and crawled towards the spot where his grandmother lay, never taking his eyes off Belchetta. By the time he got there, Granny had gone.

Suddenly, a horrible screech filled the cellar. Barnaby looked up to see Belchetta balancing on her big belly on the side of the vat. Granny had dragged herself up the ladder and had hold of Belchetta's ankle. With her last ounce of strength, she thrust the ankle into the air, and Belchetta slid head first into the tank.

Barnaby walked slowly towards the giant jar and watched as she sank down into the thick waxy vinegar. He was transfixed, unaware of his own injuries. Her already wrinkled face was creased beyond all recognition, and two hooded eyes, full of anger and resentment, glared accusingly at him. The hatred washed over his body like a bucket of icy water. He slumped to his knees, disgusted but fascinated, and stared back at what now resembled a large and demented pickled walnut.

He tried to look away, but realized with a jolt that he couldn't. Granny had been right – pickling was in his blood, and he had just been involved in the darkest pickling of all.

"Pickled bogle," Granny said, weakly. "Now *that* is dark."

CHAPTER 32
Final Words

Granny Hogsflesh slid down the ladder and collapsed in a heap at the bottom.

Barnaby ran to her, his arms streaked with blood from the cuts the rope had made.

Her skin was turning grey and crispy. She was withering before his eyes.

"Granny," said Barnaby. "What can I do?"

"Forgive me," she whispered.

"Of course I forgive you," he said. "You fought for us; you fought for *all* of us, Dad too."

"Go and get him for me, Barnaby."

Barnaby untied his parents and the three of

them gathered around Granny on the floor.

"I don't expect you to ever forgive me," she breathed.

"Mother, you mustn't talk," said Mum, tearfully. "You must save your strength."

"It's too late for that, Hatty. Nothing can save me. I was a stupid old fool who wanted to control everybody. Please say you will forgive me. Especially you, Fergus."

She turned her sunken face towards Barnaby's dad.

"I'm trying," he said, uncertainly, "but I am still cursed with the bogle's beard."

"The curse meant nothing. You could have broken it any time you wanted, instead of setting off on a madcap adventure."

"What do you mean?"

"The answer is right beside you; it always has been," she said, her voice growing fainter. "You needed a kiss from a bogle. Hatty is part bogle, you great oaf."

Dad let out a sigh of relief as Mum stood up and gave him a kiss on the lips. Barnaby looked away in disgust.

"Yuck," he said. "Isn't there any other way?"

"Barnaby," croaked Granny. "Come close. There is not much breath left in my body and I have to talk to you."

"No, Granny, please rest."

"You were right," she said, ignoring his request. "The dark pickling is bad. It serves me right to be brought down by my own pickles."

She was finding it hard to talk now and her voice was barely a whisper.

"You will become a great pickler, and so I leave you my precious factory and everything in it. But Barnaby, you must destroy the dark pickles before they destroy you. Don't make the same mistakes I did. I know you will do the right thing. You're a good boy."

Barnaby found her hand and she gave his a weak squeeze.

His mum and dad sat on the floor beside them.

"When you sank into the bog, I thought about what I had done," said Granny. "I felt so guilty and awful, and I decided to change my ways. I didn't go straight home, but went off to buy something special to make it up to you. That is why I wasn't in the house when Belchetta arrived." She managed a smile. "It's up in the kitchen."

"What is?" asked Barnaby.

Granny could hardly talk now and he leaned over to catch her final words. But her hand dropped away from his, and with a final big rumble of wind, her eyes closed and her head fell to one side.

CHAPTER 33
The Silver Flask

Mum let out a huge sob and cradled her mother's head in her arms. Barnaby looked on helplessly. He couldn't believe how awful he felt. He had grown strangely fond of his granny during the time they had spent together. He hadn't even apologized for accusing her of pickling his dad. And now she had given her life to save theirs.

"There must be something we can do," wailed Mum. "She can't be killed by a toenail. Call an ambulance."

Dad put his arm around her. "I'm sorry, Hatty, but it's too late," he said. "There aren't any medicines that can save her now."

"Wait!" cried Barnaby. He stood up and ran over to the beetroot section. "Granny was given some medicine. She said it was an antidote for ninety per cent of poisons."

He started flinging jars of beetroot off the shelves.

"Dad, help me!" he shouted. "We're looking for a tiny silver flask."

Dad rushed over and pulled the jars off the higher shelves whilst Barnaby worked furiously below him.

"It's too late," sobbed Mum, still cradling her mother. "She's gone."

Finally Barnaby saw a glint of silver on the lowest shelf. He threw the flask to his mum, who caught it and immediately unplugged the top.

"How much do I use?" she asked, her hands shaking.

"Just pour it all in!" he shouted. "What have we got to lose?"

The liquid pouring into Granny's mouth was as silver as the flask it came in. When every last drop had gone, they stared at the motionless figure, willing her to move. But after what seemed like a lifetime, Barnaby felt his dad's hands gently helping him up.

"Come on, son," he said. "We can't do any more."

Dad led Barnaby and his mum towards the door, Mum sobbing quietly. Then from behind them a loud rumble like thunder rattled through the cellar. They turned to see Granny Hogsflesh sitting up, her cheeks wobbling with the force of a huge belch.

"Better out than in," she croaked.

Barnaby and Mum ran back, flinging their arms around her.

"Get off me, you great twits," she yelled, but Barnaby could see the smile in her eyes. Her grey hair had turned silver and, apart from her skin, which now had a soft metallic sheen, she appeared to be completely recovered.

"I feel fantastic," she said, studying her silvery arms.

"And you look very . . . um . . . shiny," said Mum.

Dad hung back, but Granny beckoned him over.

"Help me up, Fergus," she said, holding her arms up to him. He pulled her to her feet and helped her into a chair. The three of them stood around her.

"I have been a silly old woman," she said. "I misjudged Barnaby and maybe I have misjudged you too. I thought you had abandoned your family when you found out about their bogle ancestry, but now I know you would never do that." She paused and looked Barnaby's dad up and down. "You may well look like a gormless tramp, but Hatty obviously sees something in you."

Dad frowned. "I. . ." he began, but Granny carried on over him.

"And so what if you have a brain the size of one of your horrible little peas? You are a good father to Barnaby."

Dad opened his mouth to speak again, but couldn't think of anything to say, so stood there with his mouth hanging open. Barnaby and his mum glanced anxiously at each other, but Granny carried on, oblivious.

"I have been brought back from the brink of death, and that changes the way you think about life. Fergus, if you wish to go back to pea picking, then you are as stupid as you look. However, I will not stand in your way again. I now understand that you don't want me bossing you about and interfering in your life. But things have changed, I have changed, and if you are willing, I need your help."

"Go on. . ." said Dad, recovering slightly.

"I am going to try and close down the dark side of pickling," she said, gesturing around the cellar. "It's not going to be easy; it's a very tempting business to be in, very lucrative. There are going to be a lot of unhappy clients, and believe me, they are not the type of people you want to upset. But I know that Barnaby doesn't agree with it." She gave Barnaby's hand a pat as she spoke. "So I am willing to try and turn my back on it." She gave a big sigh as she looked around at all her work.

"Maybe we should just keep the animal gases," she said, quietly.

"No," said Barnaby, firmly.

"No, of course not, you're right. We need to build upon the special pickles, the bold pickles." Her voice was rising. "The LIFE-CHANGING PICKLES . . . THE PICKLES OF THE FUTURE," she shouted.

Everyone looked slightly alarmed, but Granny managed to calm herself. She cleared her throat.

"What do you think, Fergus?"

"I don't think you need the help of a pea-brained, gormless tramp," said Dad.

Granny's face dropped and the two of them glared at each other. Barnaby stepped in between them.

"How about if we pickle Dad's peas?" he said brightly.

Granny pulled a face, and Dad still looked doubtful. Mum put her arm around his waist and smiled up at him.

"I think that's a great idea," she said. "Fresh meets pickled."

"It sounds revolting," said Granny, "but for the sake of Barnaby and Hatty, I'm willing to give it a try if you are, Fergus."

Dad looked down at Barnaby's and Mum's hopeful faces.

"We would have to live in our own home," he said, cautiously.

"What, that horrible little sha—?" Granny stopped herself. ". . .OK."

"And Barnaby couldn't work with you all the time; he has to go to school."

"Naturally," she said. "I don't want him becoming a pea brain."

Dad paused for a moment, thinking hard. "But if Hatty and Barnaby want to, then I suppose if we took it day by day, we could come to some arrangement."

Granny leapt from her chair. "Wonderful!" she cried.

Barnaby couldn't help smiling. With Mum and Dad there too, he was quite looking forward to his new pickling pastime. He even had some ideas of his own. Maybe he was born to pickle.

Granny led them to the door. "Time for a celebration," she said.

Barnaby hesitated.

"Just before you nearly died, you said there was something in the kitchen. What is it?"

"It's a bogle," she grinned.

CHAPTER 34
A New Bogle

Barnaby lagged behind his family. Just when he thought everything was going to be OK, he had to face another bogle.

"I don't think I'm ready to meet another bogle just yet," he said.

"Nonsense," said Granny, pushing through the kitchen doors. They all followed cautiously. Granny stood in the middle of the room, smiling broadly. She gestured towards the kitchen table. Barnaby slowly crouched down and peered under it. There, curled up in a basket and fast asleep, was a puppy.

"He's a cross between a boxer and a beagle – a bogle," she said.

Barnaby laughed out loud, partly with happiness, partly with relief. He picked up the dozy puppy, who woke up and gave his cheek a sleepy lick.

"Thank you, Granny," he said, burying his face into the soft fur.

"You enjoy him, Barnaby," she said. "I hope this little dog will be as loyal and faithful to you as you are to your family. You have a stubborn streak, just like your mother. You never gave up on your dad and you were right not to. I can see now that he loves you and your mum, just like your grandpa – God pickle his soul – loved me."

Barnaby looked at his grandmother's shining face. It wasn't just the silver sheen which made it glow, there was something more. Mum noticed it too.

"I think your human half has triumphed over your bogle half, Mother," she said.

"Maybe," said Granny, "but things are never black and white, Hatty. Humans are not all good and bogles are not all bad. They are surly, stubborn creatures, but they can fight for what they believe in. We have bogle blood running through our veins, and I think it shows. We must learn to accept it and use it to our advantage."

Maybe the bogle in me has shown itself, thought Barnaby. He certainly felt that he had the courage to face anything now. He might still be a short, quiet boy, but now he could say boo to a goose. In fact, he could say boo to a whole flock of geese. He scratched the puppy behind his ears, which made him wag his tail madly.

"I'm going to call him Morley," he said, "after Mary Morley. It was her diary that was supposed to bring this family down, but it actually brought us all together. Now we have the chance to make the *Ho-flay* Pickle Company something great."

Granny Hogsflesh belched proudly as Mum and Dad put their arms around him.

Morley, the newest bogle in the family leapt from Barnaby's arms into Granny's and licked her surprised face.

"The Curse of the Bogle's Beard will never be a problem again," chuckled Barnaby. "From now on we're going to get plenty of bogle kisses."

The End . . .
(or is it?*)